# Blind Faith

## by

## Susan Payne

**Blind Faith**

The Wild Rose Press, Inc.
PO Box 708
Adams Basin, NY 14410-0708
Visit us at www.thewildrosepress.com

Publishing History
First Rose Edition, 2020
Trade Paperback ISBN 978-1-5092-3413-4
Digital ISBN 978-1-5092-3414-1

Published in the United States of America

Cassie took in his pallor, his despondent pose, and his breakfast still waiting to be eaten sitting next to him on a rough wooden table.

Hesitantly, she said softly so as not to startle him, "Christopher, it's me, Cassie. I've come because you asked for me."

Christopher's head snapped up, facing where she stood and he seemed paler than even before. "Oh, Cassie. I-I'm sorry. I'm so sorry. I didn't know what to tell them. I-I was having a bad time and they asked for my fiancée's name, and I didn't want to tell them, you know… I didn't know what to say so I finally gave them your name." By this time there were tears running from under the bandage and Cassie went to the bed sitting on the edge. Trying to give him comfort.

She bent to put her cheek against Christopher's, getting as close as she dare without hurting him, to let him know where she was and that she wasn't upset he called for her.

"Shush. Shush. It's going to be all right. I'm here with you now. It's all right, anything you said, it's all right. I don't care. I'm here now and that is all that matters. Oh, my poor boy, what have they done to you?" she whispered. Cassie found herself rocking, holding the little brother she always wanted, crying in her arms.

## Dedication

To my family who have always shown such faith in me.
My love is with them always.

England 1814

# CHAPTER ONE

Cassie stood up brushing back a strand of hair dislodged from her once neat chignon, the starched white cap she usually wore long-gone in the bushes. Expelling a deep sigh, she bent over crooning softly to the injured dog laying half hidden in the undergrowth. "There, there, sweet thing. You'll feel so much better if you would let me help you. I know you're hurt, but I can fix that, I really can."

Repeating the soothing sounds, the large golden dog finally seemed to relax, but still watched her with large worried eyes. Slowly reaching out, Cassie smoothed down the animal's coat, trying to find any broken bones or torn skin. When she got to the hind quarters, the dog whimpered and tried to move further into the brush. "Oh, so that is where it hurts. I see a little blood there, too. Poor boy, you must have been hit while chasing a carriage. Don't you know by now, you can't catch those whirling wheels?"

With a stream of nonsensical talk, she tried to distract the animal from the pain she caused it while slowly sliding the burlap bag under the dog's body. It was the only way she was going to get the poor thing to the cart and then home to give it some much needed medical care.

"Hey, you there, hiding in the bushes. Show yourself or I'll call a constable to find out why you're about," a man shouted from the roadway.

Cassie's first thought was, *drat, can't anyone mind their own business? What if I was relieving myself?* She stifled a giggle at the thought of the expression on the man's face if she were to shout back, she was indeed, doing just that.

She found herself saying, "Instead of demanding what I am doing, why don't you come in and help me? I am trying to give aid to an injured dog and a little male strength would not come amiss."

Cassie expected to hear a carriage or horse continue on but within moments, there was a thrashing through the brush behind her. A very large, somewhat exasperated man immerged straightening his fine coat and firmly pushing his hat onto his head to keep it from falling off. He was extremely good looking with dark hair brushing his shirt collar and piercing grey eyes, which made one think he was reading ones every thought.

The gentleman gave a small head bow and said shortly, "Quinn Lancaster, Earl of Hedley, Viscount of Langley, at your service."

Cassie hoped her mouth remained closed. It was just her luck to run into someone who might know her aunt. She certainly didn't want it getting about London that she met with strange men in the woods but couldn't resist pulling the tiger's tail.

Dipping into a court curtsey, she replied, "Queen Elizabeth, my lord." She rose facing him quite aware of how she must appear in her soiled day-dress, wellingtons, and long leather gloves tied at her shoulders to protect her sleeves from things such as this.

She turned to indicate the dog that was becoming agitated by the stranger. "I'll take the bitey end if you help lift the other. I hope to move him without causing him too much pain."

Lord Hedley went to his assigned end, unbuttoned his coat and bent down to grasp the corners of the bag. Together they shuffled slowly toward the roadside, Cassie going backwards through the hedge.

"I could simply pick him up, you know. It would be much faster," the man said.

"No, that could cause more injuries. He may have internal bleeding or a broken bone could pierce an organ. It will be best to keep him as flat as possible."

"Good Lord, how do you know all that? I take it this isn't your dog so who is going to take care of him once we get him out of here?"

"I don't recognize him from around here. He may have followed a carriage for miles before being struck by the wheels. I'll have to fix him up and find him a good home."

Cassie finally emerged from the underbrush finding herself at the edge of the road where her dogcart and an enclosed carriage stood. Its driver tried not to gape at them as they appeared from the brush. A well-bred horse with an expensive leather saddle was tied to the rear of the carriage.

Lord Hedley raised the cloth high enough to slide her patient, bag and all, onto the dogcart.

Cassie laughed at herself as she tried to make some semblance of her dress and hair, feeling it tumble completely out of the pins that had held it in some sort of style when she left home that morning. She saw him staring at the dog cart in indecision. "It doesn't escape my sense of the ludicrous to realize I will be pulling a dog in a dog cart."

He suggested with visible hesitation, "I could put the dog into my carriage and bring him home for you."

"Thank you, my lord, you have been more than courteous. The dog will be much more comfortable in the slower paced cart." Cassie stepped between the narrow wood slats that usually held a dog. "I can miss any ruts in the road to lessen his pain."

Giving a little nod, Lord Hedley mounted his horse. "As you wish." With a call to the carriage driver they both rode away leaving Cassie to pull her patient home.

The trip home was uneventful until she came into view of the cottage she shared with her aunt and saw the same carriage and horse standing in front of it. Cassie felt a rush of heat rise from the roots of her hair. She thought by not introducing herself she would remain an unknown entity to the lofty lord yet here he was, probably relaying the whole event, including her looking like someone dragged through a hedge backwards, to her Aunt Laura.

Not that Aunt Laura would care. She certainly didn't stand on ceremony and gave up caring what polite society says one should or should not do long ago. That is only one of the areas where she and her aunt agreed so well. Abandoning their titles, learning to live without a bevy of servants, and definitely not needing a man's name to live a productive life.

Since Cassie had a patient, she continued to wheel the cart through the garden entrance and to the building where the injured dog would finally find relief from his pain.

Leaving the dog on the cart, she began assembling the medical items she felt would be required to mend the dog, including the sharp bladed saw. She sensed him before seeing the large shadow blocking out the sunshine coming through the shed's open door.

Cassie turned to see Lord Hedley who gave her a crooked grin. "Miss Cassandra Woods, I presume? Your aunt said you would be here. I did not expect to see you again, and never thought to ask if you were indeed the person, I was in Littleton to find." He bent to enter the low doorway then stood to his full height, which seemed much more intimidating in the enclosed space then it had alongside the road.

Washing her hands in water from a bucket, she pulled on clean gardening gloves. "Well, you can come in handy again. Take this bottle and try not to breathe it in or get it on any of your clothing. Now let a few drops fall onto this cone and hold it over the dog's muzzle. It will put him to sleep and then I can see how badly broken this leg is."

Lord Hedley, without bothering to ask or argue, did as Cassie directed. Once the animal was asleep, Cassie felt along the dog's hind leg with sure hands then gave it a quick yank followed by a push.

"That went better than I thought," she said as she smoothed her hands along the dog's rear end and tied the two back legs together. "The leg was merely pulled out of the socket. If we can keep him down for a little while it should be fine, just sore. These other cuts are superficial and I'll clean them before he wakes up."

Once Lord Hedley was relieved of his duties, he

glared at the woman in front of him. "Miss Woods, I must say I find your care of a dumb animal admirable, but incongruous with your lack of care about a man to whom you were once betrothed."

Cassie glanced up at the man, but returned to quietly cleaning the dog's wounds. Lord Hedley was obviously agitated. His hands were thrust behind him and his mouth grim. She could see the man had come a long distance and was having difficulty keeping his emotions under control. She wondered who had sent him and why after all these years would the ton decide she was worthy of their notice once again.

"I know it is difficult for a pretty young woman to contemplate living with a husband who has come back from the Peninsular less than perfect, but I think your treatment of Christopher Moore is abominable. Totally beneath the pale." He finished with righteous indignation.

Alert to anything the man might say, she asked casually, "So your visit is about Chris, umm, Christopher?"

"Yes, of course. These men volunteer to protect our shores, our way of life and for you to then turn him away because he comes back blind, when he needs his family and loved ones' support the most. For you to break your betrothal, ignore his letters and pleas, turn away from him…well, it is beyond conceivable to me. You should be ashamed of your treatment of a fine gentleman."

The man in front of her was obviously emotional and with every accusation the color of his face deepened. Cassie was intrigued and alarmed at what she was discerning from his words.

Standing, she faced her aggressor. "You are right in

that Christopher deserves better. But you are sure he asked for me to come?"

"Of course, I am. I asked him outright and he gave me both your name and direction."

"Then I think you are correct. When our young men go off to war, to protect our way of life and put themselves in harm's way, we at home, must be available to give any aid we can. Where is he? I will leave immediately."

Lord Hedley seemed taken back at Cassie's quick acquiescence as he stammered, "I-I brought a carriage. I planned on accompanying you to Hedley Hall myself, riding my own horse, of course."

"How did Christopher come to be at Hedley Hall? I'm not sure I understand," Cassie asked now as she put together possibilities. He was wounded and that alone raised her emotions, knowing he asked for her was all she needed to be on her way. Her mind buzzed with the need for expediency, but knew she would have to wait for daylight before she could go to him.

There was a hesitation as Lord Hedley seemed to deliberate on how much he wanted to divulge. "My brother, Nathan, returned from Spain with a head injury that caused total blindness. He became listless and pushed everyone away trying to bury himself in the darkness. I found a London doctor who was doing great things with men returning with similar injuries. Trying to convince him to come to Hedley Hall to treat my brother, he said he would with the proviso I brought other wounded soldiers with eye injuries to him as well. I found that no hardship. It was the least I could do in payment for his help. I have cleared out a wing of the manor and hired additional staff, some ex-batmen, to help with their care. The doctor suggested reuniting the men with their families and loved ones would aid those men in healing quicker and going home. We acknowledge many may not be able to regain their sight. My brother was an exception. I thank God and Dr. Landon every day for his recovery."

"Has Christopher's mother been told? She lives not far from here."

"Lieutenant Moore asked we not contact her since he feels she is too frail and the news her only son is blind may be too much for her to take."

"Yes," agreed Cassie. "She hasn't been well this last winter. I visit her every week, but a, ah, friend has moved in so there is someone with her to tend to her needs."

"I'll return tomorrow morning, if that meets your approval. We will be at Hedley Hall by nightfall barring any unforeseen events, such as finding an injured dog along the road." He gave Cassie a lopsided grin again with just a hint of those attractive dimples. She tamped down the pleasant feelings this man created in her. She had given up his way of life years ago never wishing to live so frivolously again.

"I'll be ready. Would you care to stay for dinner? I'm sure my aunt would have me extend the invitation."

"Actually, your aunt already offered the invitation, but I think it best if I go into Littleton so the horses can find a stable and my driver and I can get rooms for the night." With that he said, "Good night, Miss Woods."

Cassie dropped into a curtsey. "My lord."

Quinn rode on in quiet thought, following the carriage without really seeing the scenery or noting the homes they passed. The oxymoron of a beautiful young woman nursing a myriad number of animals, yet ignoring a man she once was engaged to made him angry. He noted on the way to the building where he was told he could find Miss Woods, there had been numerous small cages housing assorted animals. A rabbit with its front foot bandaged, a cat without a tail, and then there was the dog with one of its hind legs missing, an ear chewed off, one eye and half a tail, probably named, Lucky. How did she come to be the caregiver for so many, including her aunt if he wasn't mistaken, and still break her betrothal and her betrothed's heart?

It didn't help his bad humor that he found Miss Woods attractive and funny. She could laugh at herself and he found that appealing, too. When he had pushed through the bushes to come upon a beautiful woodnymph his chest tightened and his breathing quickened. He found himself sinking into her sherry colored eyes and would have sworn there was a halo-like glow around her golden-brown hair. But all that was shattered by the very real girl who laughed at him. He could tell she took great amusement in his discomfiture.

He had to keep himself from smiling at her taunting of her betters with that curtsey. Standing there in a filthy dress with her hair tumbling down around her shoulders. He wanted to pull the rest of the pins out and let the silky tresses slide through his fingers. Shaking his head to clear it, he knew that kind of thinking would get him in all sorts of hot water.

He must remember she was a heartless flirt who broke-off a long-standing agreement with an exemplary young man such as Lieutenant Moore merely because he had been wounded. She acted as if she hadn't even known of his injuries. In fact, she hadn't asked about the extent of his injuries at all when requested to visit young

Moore.

Was she saying she would visit Hedley Hall so as not to appear badly to society? To him? Well, it didn't matter as long as she saw Moore and that the Lieutenant was given the opportunity to tell her what he thought of her. After Moore had his say, Cassandra Woods would be put back into the carriage and sent home. Perhaps then, Lieutenant Moore would be able to heal both physically and mentally.

Cassie was trying to assemble items she felt she might need for the trip. She would tell Ben, the handyman who cared for the cottage, to refill those jars of herbs and salves that were now depleted. She would also tell him to take care of Aunt Laura, although that wasn't necessary since he always made himself available and was at her aunt's beck and call. The box she filled was heavy and well packed with cotton batting and bandages both to protect items from breaking and to be used if needed.

In the house, she informed her aunt of the events since they had last been together.

Following Cassie as she grabbed her sewing basket and other items off the shelves in the parlor, Aunt Laura asked worriedly, "Why would Christopher give Lord Hedley your name as his betrothed? Do you think he has a head injury and has gotten confused? What about Lucy? She will be crushed if Christopher has forgotten her and their betrothal. Should we tell Lucy and have you take her with you? Perhaps seeing her will help Christopher remember." The old woman stopped in her tracks with her fingers to her quivering lips. "Oh, Cassie, this doesn't sound good at all."

"I know, but I promise to let you know what is

happening as soon as possible. We can decide if Lucy and Mrs. Moore should be told after I speak with Chris." Cassie perused the books on the shelves in the well-furnished parlor before selecting a few. "Aunt Laura, I think I'll eat later. Have Sarah make up a plate for me, please. I want to pack and get around some things I think I might need. At least Chris is alive and must be well enough for visitors or Lord Hedley wouldn't have ridden all this way to get me." Cassie knew her aunt was as fond of Christopher as she was and tried to relieve her of some concern.

"Yes, we must look at the brighter side and pray you can help Christopher through this terrible time. If there is anything you need…," the older woman began but trailed off, ending the conversation with a worried expression.

"I know. I can always trust in you." Cassie held her skirts up as she rushed up the narrow staircase to her bedroom.

The next morning Cassie heard the crunch of wheels in the stones as the carriage pulled up in front of the cottage. Tugging on her gloves, she checked the mirror to make sure her green hat with its little feathered bird perched as if in a nest sat forward on her head. It was a gift from a grateful cat lover after the cat swallowed yarn, which then became lodged in its intestine.

She wore her forest green carriage dress, trimmed with black braiding. The high neck and tight sleeves made less opportunity for the inevitable dust when traveling to stick to her skin. Like all her clothes, it had been expensive and well-made when she wore it during her first season five years ago.

Cassie met Lord Hedley as he stepped onto the front

porch. He bowed and greeted her and she dipped a small curtsey. "Good morning, my lord."

If Hedley was surprised she didn't travel with a maid, he didn't show it. After all, he thought she was simply a girl from Littleton. He would have to get used to her lifestyle or not. She didn't alter her life for any man. Except Christopher, she would do anything for him.

She indicated the worn wooden box and small travelling trunk for the driver to carry to the carriage explaining the need for care with the box since it contained glass. Cassie thanked him and let Lord Hedley help her into the carriage. That was the last communication they shared until they stopped for the noonday meal at an inn which was clean and efficient.

Lord Hedley asked for and received a private parlor, a substantial luncheon and pot of tea. All of which Cassie approved of. There was little talk between Lord Hedley and her during the meal. Cassie not having any more questions Lord Hedley could answer and Lord Hedley in deep thought about things that evidently didn't include Cassie.

She had spent all morning in deep thought. She was past the questions of why her, why Christopher had asked for her instead of Lucy or his mother. Whatever the reason, whether on purpose or not, she was the one coming to his side. The boy who made her summers so much more fun, allowing her to be who she was without questioning the correctness. Never judging her or comparing her to other young girls of society.

Cassie took this opportunity to use the facilities for ladies and was back at the carriage door ready to begin the second half of the trip by the time Lord Hedley paid the proprietor. He mounted his large horse and they continued toward his home.

Hedley's thoughts kept returning to the woman in his carriage. He was surprised at how much time he spent thinking about her as he rode back toward his home. He questioned his motives in bringing Miss Woods back with him. She wasn't exactly as he had pictured her. He expected a self-centered miss with feathers for brains focused on new dresses and gossip from London. Cassandra Woods seemed to be the exact opposite. Did he do wrong not to warn her of what was to come? Of how he spent hours listening to Moore rant against her betrayal. That Moore was aware of her lack of loyalty. That Moore knew his betrothed continued with her life after he was sent to the Peninsular as if she were a free woman to give her affections as she may. Moore told him he had proof.

The story wasn't new, Hedley thought. It was just so much more dangerous, so much eviler, when the man involved sustained such a life altering injury. He had seen men, broken by war, but killed by the actions of loved ones left safe at home. Suicide was a real danger to these men. At least Nathan had been stopped before he could do himself an injury. One of the drawbacks of being blind was one did not know if one was visible to others.

Now with the hard work of Dr. Landon and Nathan's fiancée, Melanie, who refused to abandon Nathan even when he was pushing her away, even when he said awful, hurtful things to her Nathan had recovered. Melanie held tight to their commitment and in the end, it led to Nathan's acceptance of his disability and a happy marriage.

Hedley didn't think this would be the outcome for Moore who was adamant about his betrothed's perfidy. It was Dr. Landon who sent Hedley seeking Moore's ex-fiancée. The doctor thought if Moore could rid himself of the pain caused by this unthinking young lady, Moore might then look toward at least trying to get better. It was a gamble, but better a selfish miss being put on the carpet for her thoughtlessness than a man losing his soul as well as his life.

He had no interest in hearing Moore tear Miss Woods apart, but he must follow through with this plan. Dr. Landon thought it would be the best medicine for Moore and sometimes medicine was difficult to swallow.

As night fell, Cassie realized they must be approaching Hedley Hall. The carriage turned onto a graveled drive from the quieter sand road. She was still able to make out the silhouette of a large, three-storied house with a central section and two large wings, the one on the right appearing to be a little newer than the other. There were lights in the windows on the west side, but the east wing was dark appearing as if it wasn't in use, yet there was the most activity at that end of the house.

Off the east side there were numerous groupings of tents and even a small campfire. Cassie could make out the shapes of men, probably the soldiers Lord Hedley spoke about. There were so many more than she thought there would be. Could all these men be blind? All these men facing a life without ever seeing their families again?

The carriage came to a stop in front of the graceful stairs leading up to the wide front door. A footman lowered the step and helped Cassie down. She turned as

Lord Hedley approached with an offer to accompany her into the house.

"Could I be excused from dinner, please? I feel a little tired and find I may not be a very good guest," she explained as they entered the brightly lit foyer.

Lord Hedley bowed. "I'll have someone take you up to your room. I'm sure the maid can bring you a plate and, of course, tea. A footman can show you the breakfast room in the morning. Have a good night."

"Thank you, my lord. I look forward to seeing Christopher in the morning." She curtsied before following a young maid up one side of the curved staircase.

She changed into her nightclothes as soon as her trunk arrived to her room. The maid brought up a light supper and a pot of tea Cassie was pleased to see. She had a lot to think about and was anxious to talk with Chris. Something wasn't right and she was hoping it was more a misunderstanding on Lord Hedley's part and not a serious brain injury on Christopher's.

# CHAPTER TWO

Cassie chose to wear a simple day dress without a lot of lace or trim and arrived at the breakfast room early. Lord Hedley, his brother, Colonel Nathan Lancaster, and the Colonel's wife, Lady Melanie, were already there. Lord Hedley made their introductions. She accepted the plate Lord Hedley filled for her as she sat at one of the empty chairs and proceeded to eat.

She discreetly observed how Lady Melanie aided Colonel Lancaster with his meal, but he didn't seem to need much help. He was able to feed himself and felt for his cup with slow, deliberate movements alongside his plate. If one did not know his incapacity, one wouldn't notice the slight hesitations.

The Colonel must have felt the need to explain. "I have been blessed with partial vision after several months of total darkness. I was tested and found worthy by my Maker. My sight is best in daylight so we get up early to lengthen the time I have to see my beautiful wife." He turned toward his blushing wife. "I see mostly shadows, dark against light, but some colors have been appearing and I can make out other outlines, especially in bright sun. I am hoping it continues to get better, but if this is all I have, then I will be thankful for what I have been given."

Optimistic, Cassie said, "That sounds extremely encouraging. I hope the other soldiers progress as well." She finished by saying, "If you would excuse me, I am anxious to talk with Christopher, er, Lieutenant Moore.

Can a footman point me in the right direction?"

The gentlemen stood when Cassie rose to leave and Lord Hedley said, sounding as if he wished to be anywhere but escorting her, "I will take you to him."

The tap of their shoes was the only sound between them as they crossed the black and white marble squares of the foyer and out the front door. They turned left toward the tents.

Lord Hedley explained, "Many of the men are bivouacked in the tents. Some cannot get used to being inside after sleeping under canvas for so many months while others cannot manage the doorways and walls of an enclosed area. I'll take you to the Lieutenant's pavilion. He is in a sort of hospital ward."

Lord Hedley walked slower as they reached the outside perimeter of the shelters. He pointed to a row of beds. "Lieutenant Moore is in the third cot from the end. I wish you the best."

Cassie turned back to him, a little confused with his parting words, and smiled. "I will be fine. We have to worry about Christopher now." With that she walked quickly toward the bed pointed out to her.

Taking no notice of the other beds or their occupants, she was focusing on the cot with Christopher's blond curls showing above white bandages wrapped around the top half of his head. His right arm was in a sling with the hand wrapped like a mummy with fresh blood still seeping through the gauze. Cassie took in his pallor, his despondent pose, and his breakfast still waiting to be eaten sitting next to him on a rough wooden table.

Hesitantly, Cassie said softly so as not to startle him, "Christopher, it's me, Cassie. I've come because you asked for me."

Christopher's head snapped up, facing where she stood and he seemed paler than even before. "Oh, Cassie. I-I'm sorry. I'm so sorry. I didn't know what to tell them. I-I was having a bad time and they asked for my fiancée's name, and I didn't want to tell them, you know… I didn't know what to say so I finally gave them your name." By this time there were tears running from under the bandage and Cassie went to the bed sitting on the edge. Trying to give him comfort.

"Christopher, you can't think that Lucy hasn't been true to you. She is worried sick only acting as if everything is normal for your mother's sake. We should write and let them know…"

His hand squeezed hers. "I made up stories so that they wouldn't contact my family. I told them horrible things about L-Lucy simply so they would quit pestering me about informing her I was still alive…"

"Lucy would want to know, Christopher. You know she would and so would your mother. They both love you so much."

"And that's why they must not know I'm back in England wounded as I am. I can't face the disappointment. Letting them see me this way. Knowing I'll never be a man for them to depend upon."

"Don't speak like that. Even if you never recover your eye-sight, they love you."

"No. Don't let anyone know about me. How I am. I'll never be the man they need me to be. I can't face them as I am. It is better this way."

She bent to put her cheek against Christopher's, getting as close as she dare without hurting him, to let him know where she was and that she wasn't upset he called for her.

"Shush. Shush. It's going to be all right. I'm here with you now. It's all right, anything you said, it's all right. I don't care. I'm here now and that is all that matters. Oh, my poor boy, what have they done to you?" she whispered. Cassie found herself rocking, holding Christopher, the little brother she always wanted, crying in her arms.


From several yards away, Quinn watched the couple, so obviously in love begin the healing. He hadn't thought this reunion was going to end this way, but perhaps it was for the best. There was a small nagging at the back of his mind, a smoldering bit of anger at a woman who could treat a man she promised to honor with such disregard. But if Moore wanted to forgive her and accept her with all her flaws, who was he to tell him, nay? Quinn gazed over to the tent one last time before turning back to the manor house. He had correspondence to see to and wouldn't need to take the trip back to Littleton to return Cassandra Woods into her aunt's care that day.

Cassie straightened to a sitting position on the bed and wiped the tear tracks from Christopher's cheek. Embarrassed by such a show of emotion, Christopher said, "Some soldier I make. Turning into a watering-pot because a friend comes to visit me in hospital."

"Do you remember the funerals we held for all those poor animals I couldn't save? We would dig a grave, and line it with flowers and cry over every single one of them. I always do the same thing to this day. The loss of a life, the loss of a promise not fulfilled. I always think the tears help wash away the sorrow. Cleanses the soul like rain cleans the air of dust. I think crying is sometimes the best medicine for a broken heart. And my heart was breaking seeing you in this bed all alone."

"I'm sorry, Cassie, I mean, Lady Cassandra. I never meant for you to become involved. I didn't know they were going to fetch you. But thank God you came. I don't know what I would have done if they had brought Lucy."

"We are more as equals now than at any other time in our lives and you used to always call me, Cassie, when we ran over the fields together."

"Yes, but I was still in short pants and you were in pig tails. You went off to London and got all the blokes to offer for you. Then you turned them all down and went to veterinary school instead. That showed them all where they stood." He teased her as the old Chris would have done.

Cassie smiled and noted Christopher was already sounding like the young boy she remembered laughing with and there was a little healthy color in his cheeks.

"You didn't eat your breakfast and luncheon is being brought around," Cassie announced.

"I can't eat without help and there aren't enough batmen. I hate to think what I look like. When I try to feed myself, I most often get an empty spoon to my mouth. I don't know if it starts out that way or dribbles all down myself on the way there."

Cassie said with a laugh, "Well, I can't tell what you were supposed to have for dinner last night so that probably means the spoon was empty in the first place. But you are much too thin and even an animal doctor knows that a good recovery is based on good meals.

Let's see what's for luncheon."

A footman was pushing around a cart with a large pot and piles of metal bowls and spoons. A man in uniform was filling the bowls and passing them around. Cassie accepted one for Christopher.

"Hmmm, a soup, rather thin but appears as if it was made with a good stock. Let's see." Cassie reached over, dumped out the cold tea from the metal cup next to the bed and filled it with the still warm soup. "There," she said as she handed the cup into Christopher's good hand. "Be careful, it's hot."

Christopher said as if surprised, "I can tell. The cup is hot on the outside."

Cassie studied the cup thinking. "Yes, it would be. I bet you can tell how full it is too by the difference in the heat from the bottom of the cup to the rim."

Christopher replied, "Probably, but I intend to get some of this soup in me for a change and we can figure out your theories later. I suppose you plan on doing experiments upon everything I do and everything I need to do? Please, I beg you, leave me some privacy. You were always worse than my nursemaid."

"Oh Christopher, I've gotten much better about those things. I learned everything at school so I won't ask you embarrassing questions about how little boys are made." She teased him happily noticing his cheeks redden. She continued, "Don't worry, no one is close enough to hear me. Besides, you were always like my little brother. I think I even remember helping to change your nappy."

"Oh Lord, I had forgotten your wicked sense of humor. I don't know if I can live through this. Perhaps it is just as well I can't see you take glee in my chagrin. I should never have given your name to the doctor. This is going to be my undoing." But he smiled in his supposed misery.

When next Quinn walked over to the tents, he found Moore and Miss Woods laughing, really laughing. There were several others joining in with whatever the conversation was and they too wore wide smiles on their faces. It was something he thought he would never see among this group and his curiosity got the better of him. As he moved closer, Miss Woods picked up a letter and began reading.

"*I wanted to empress Molly so much, I paid to enter the greased pig contest to get the BIG PRIZE*, he capitalized those last two words," said Cassandra. "*Earnest Conroy brought the pigs. They were just piglets of about forty pounds or so, but was disqualified right off since he may have trained a pig before the contest so that left eight of us. We drew straws to see who would go first and so on and I was third. The first two had a lot of trouble getting the pigs even picked up, but I kept my sleeves rolled down and that helped to get a grip on the slippery skin. I got a real fast time, the best so far, but those stupid pigs started jumping right into the basket as soon as one of the contestants went to grab at them. All of us dirty as pigs ourselves and the judge, Mr. Murray from the dry goods store, called off the whole thing. Disqualified the pigs, he said, and confiscated the BIG PRIZE.* He capitalized those two words again," explained Cassandra. Then continued reading. "*For his self! And can you guess what it was? A big old pork pie! But before Mr. Murray could get out of the fenced area with the pie, the pigs all ran squealing and knocked him off his feet. Mr. Murray went up in the air and down again in the mud and the pie followed. The pigs dove for the pie and it was gone in a split second and the pie tin had a tooth hole in it so it wasn't any good either. I guess I'm going to have to find another way to impress Molly so maybe she will give me a kiss. That is all the news for now. Hurry up and get better. I want you home so Ma will stop bossing me around. Fondly your brother, Ned."*

Cassandra was wiping her eyes and chuckling. "Can you imagine? And those poor little pigs. They were merely trying to do what they thought everyone wanted them to do. You know they are one of the smartest animals. We don't give them the credit they deserve." Then she continued, "Thank you, Nate, for allowing us to enjoy your letter with you. I'll help with your return letter as soon as you are ready." Cassandra folded the paper and put it into Nate's hand.

Quinn made a note that the men were still smiling as they slowly progressed toward their own beds, making use of furniture and tent poles to help guide their way. He saw Cassandra leaning forward talking quietly with Moore. It seemed their relationship was back in good standing and Moore had forgiven his intended for any lapses.

He didn't think he would be able to be as generous and felt resentment for Moore's sake. Cassandra Woods should not be able to step back into the same place as she held prior to her loss of honor. Women should be held to as high a standard as men once a commitment had been made.

Quinn called out, "I'll walk you back to the house, Miss Woods. I would like to talk with you about your return trip."

Cassandra whispered something to Christopher then replied, "Certainly, my lord. I have a favor to ask of you, also."

Quinn graciously acceded her place. "Ladies first, Miss Woods."

"I take it you plan for me to return home soon, my lord?"

"Tomorrow, actually. I will not be able to accompany you, but I will send a groom so there should be no problem at the inn. You will be in good hands, I assure you," he said in a somewhat chilly voice. This young woman always made his hackles rise whenever she was near.

"I was hoping I could impose on your hospitality a while longer. There is a shortage of people to care for so many invalids and I wish to make sure Mr. Moore gets the best care and attention. I can see he isn't ready to be sent home, but I plan to be here when he is. I can help feed him and make sure his toilet is properly seen to. I am well able to take care of his needs."

"If you are trying to tell me that you have anticipated your vows and therefore can help Lieutenant Moore with his more intimate requirements, I feel that I am unable to agree to your remaining." His insides turned cold. He found it distasteful to even think of tolerating such behavior among the men. A woman should be waiting at home for her man.

Grinding her teeth, she replied, "I am not telling you we anticipated our vows. I am saying, as a licensed doctor of veterinary science, that I can be of service helping with Christopher's wounds as well as helping him transition into a non-sighted life."

"I cannot condone a properly brought-up unmarried lady to associate herself with all class of soldiers, most of them not ready to join society, either physically or mentally," he told her sternly.

"First you accuse me of being no better than I should be, and then you say you need to protect me from these men who have been through so much and paid so dearly. I am not a faint miss who needs such protection from reality. These men need someone to help them negotiate life and I know I can do that."

She was very convincing. He had seen her with the men and they responded favorably to having her amongst them. Should he send her away because she made him uncomfortable or should he allow her to stay and help? He was at war with himself.

As he argued with himself, Cassandra continued, "I would allow Christopher, all the men, the privacy they should require. Think of me as any other mother or sister nursing a brother. The men need someone to do little things for them like read and write letters, sew on missing buttons and tell them when they need a haircut. Which, by the way, most of them do."

"You're actually a doctor of veterinary science?"

She nodded.

"No wonder then the menagerie at your home. Well, this will be against my better judgment, but I know the staff is overworked as it is. I never anticipated this many men with eye injuries and I didn't realize ahead of time how many of the men would have multiple injuries. Just my naiveté. They seem to keep coming and not many are ready to be sent home. I hope this damn war ends soon." And realizing to whom he was speaking added, "Pardon my language, Miss Woods."

"Quite all right, my lord. I couldn't have said it better." She walked through the front doorway ahead of him.

He had a queer feeling he'd been had but wasn't quite sure if he wanted to know how she had done it.

Cassie dined with Lord Hedley, Colonel Lancaster and Lady Melanie. Dr. Landon was still in London trying to get more help from the government for the soldiers under his care. Cassie asked about writing materials since many of the men wanted to contact their families, but needed someone to write for them.

Lord Hedley told her, "I will frank the letters as soon as they are finished."

"I may find they have other needs. May I depend on your help, my lord?"

"Certainly, and I'll tell Milton, my butler, you have my full cooperation in making the men comfortable while they are here."

"Thank you. You have already done so much but the need is great and you are helping these men through a terrible ordeal," she told him honestly.

Seemingly embarrassed with her praise, Lord Hedley said, "It is the least I could do."

They all left the dining room together. Evidently the men didn't stand on ceremony and take brandy or smoke when the women left the table. Cassie took this time to say her good evenings and retired to her room to make plans for the following day.

Cassie thought through every problem she had seen that day in the pavilion. Not only were there not enough batmen to ensure the minimal personal care for each patient, the patients themselves still needed a great deal of medical care. There were bandages that needed to be changed and disposed of properly as well as some minimal treatments for recuperating muscles and limbs.

She wanted to help these men without becoming too intrusive in their treatments. Although she hadn't met him yet, she knew there was a Dr. Landon in charge of the men's medical needs. The problem was that he was more interested in their vision than their other injuries. Moving limbs and keeping active would help these men achieve full health, even if their sight never returned.

She needed to find a way to ingrain herself into the day-to-day activities without threatening Dr. Landon's authority. Placing herself beneath any male's control would be difficult for her, she knew. Having been in charge of her own life for years, taking orders was anathema to her at the best of times.

The following morning found Cassie up and into the breakfast room early. Lord Hedley was there wearing riding clothes. He stood as Cassie entered and she waved him to sit down but he stayed standing until she was seated. She asked the footman waiting to take her order, for two eggs and toasted bread while she poured tea for herself from the pot on the table.

"My lord," she began excitedly, "I have a few ideas to help the men ease into their normal lives if their sight is not returned when they are physically healed. With help, they can go home and live a life somewhat close to that which they had planned. No one can be completely unaffected by the loss of their eyesight but I think they can become confident enough to try." She peered expectantly into Lord Hedley's face.

He gazed at her, unable to believe what she was

27

saying. He was hearing her say things that he had thought. Only he was having trouble finding ways to make them come to fruition. Miss Woods seemed to think she had found a way.

All he could think to say was, "Tell me about it."

"Well, each man will react differently to learning how to do normal things. It is almost like retraining animals to learn to walk with fewer limbs than they once had. Something I am used to doing."

"Hence, the three-legged dog." He offered as an example.

Cassandra looked at him searchingly then said, "Oh, you met Bertram. Yes, he's been through quite a lot of relearning."

"So, his name isn't Lucky?" he asked and grinned at the expression she gave him.

"No, but one more injury and I'm going to rename him after a saint, preferably a very divine one," Cassandra said with a laugh. "My Lord, I would like to set up a schedule of sorts so that the men have some semblance of a day. A regimented pattern with specific times to be dressed for work or outdoor activities, times to dine and times for social evenings. I know I can get Christopher interested and others will join in as their health improves and their injuries heal."

Not waiting for his approval or response, Cassandra jumped up as soon as she finished eating. Reaching out, she snatched the folded newspaper next to his plate.

"Oh, this is wonderful, my lord. Many of the men were asking about what was happening in the 'outside world' as it is beginning to be known. I'll take any older issues you may have, too. Thank you so much, my lord." She sketched a quick curtsey and rushed away.

She left before Quinn realized that he hadn't stood-up when Cassandra had and that he let her escape with his paper, which he hadn't even opened yet.

He shook his head and laughed at himself. Cassandra Woods was much more than a wayward fiancée. As much life and excitement, she may bring to others, she might be the death of him.

Cassie relayed her plans to Christopher and his bedmates as she changed the bandage on his hand. "I have been studying the problems you all face now. Many of you are having trouble getting enough to eat so I've spoken with the cook and today we are having a thick bean broth and buttered bread. I am having the broth poured into cups to facilitate you eating. Dip the bread into it, but remember to keep the cup under your chin to catch the drips."

As the meal was brought around again by the same two batmen there were indeed metal cups in place of the bowls and spoons and the much-welcomed bread.

Once the men settled down to eat, she continued. "I have some little suggestions that may help some of you. Please remember I am here for your benefit and as bluntly honest as I will be with you, I expect the same. Such as the need for a haircut, which all of you do need. Those of you who have access to a valet upon your return home will not need to worry about the following. The rest will have to contend with taking care of yourselves in a manner that will allow you to be in polite society.

There were chuckles from the men listening which was becoming a larger and larger group. Word must be spreading there was a woman in the side tent and that she could speak to any of them. Cassie knew she would attract attention and hoped the men would pass along what she was doing there.

"Some of you will learn to shave yourselves, but for those who fear cutting your own throats or of those nearby, I would suggest selecting a stylish beard and mustache. It can be trimmed every week or two by a barber. For now, you should learn to make a habit of combing your facial hair to relieve it of any bits and pieces you will not be able to see. I understand it is a common practice among men."

She continued speaking to her captivated audience. "Lord Hedley has ordered a bathing tent set up. There will be a valet there to tend to the fire heating the water and any other needs you may have. Get the doctor's permission first. You are not to get any wound area wet. It is on a first come first serve basis, but is available until five o'clock each day except Sunday."

At that disclosure, several of the men shouted, "Hoorah!"

"Does anyone want more soup?" she asked and several took advantage of the new eating technique and asked for a second cup. "Then there is the issue of clothing. I think you will all be able to dress yourself, even tie your own cravat. My father did so without using a looking-glass because he said it confused him to see himself tying it."

Men with lowered heads nodded in agreement.

"Those with wives will not have issues with the following. I suggest the rest of you have your tailor keep the material with-in the same color family, all items going together unless you get him to mark it in some way to note what goes with what. Such as sewing an X into the inside edge of a vest and jacket to mark them as a set," she advised.

"I've known a few sighted men who could have used that advice," laughed one young man.

Cassie chuckled and continued, "Stay away from bright ceruse and canary yellow that may make a sight of one, when worn together."

The jovial sergeant said, "Oh, good pun, that. A sight of ourselves." And several others laughed with him.

Chuckling, she added, "I didn't mean it as a pun, but a sense of humor with all this will go a long way in recovering your old lives, I think.

"Now if everyone is done eating, does anyone wish to walk with me in the rose garden? We'll discuss what activities you used to do and what ones you should be able to continue doing." She stood to lead the group. As they followed her lead haltingly, the men were commenting on various things they missed being in the army and away from home.

"I suppose bird hunting is out, eh?" quipped the rather round middle-aged sergeant.

"Hmmm, shooting a rifle might be out of the running, but what do you think of shooting an arrow? It's been a little while since I held a bow, but I have an idea." She continued speaking so they could tell where she was. They all went toward the rose garden, some walking side by side and others feeling their way, on what she decided would be a daily ritual.

Once Christopher seemed to be on his way to recovery, Cassie didn't concentrate on his needs and condition knowing all these men at Hedley Hall would have a long and difficult journey. One young man in particular, caught her attention because he reminded her so much of Chris when he was a few years younger. My God, she thought, how young did they recruit these men?

Getting closer to him, she saw he wasn't much more than a boy.

"Hello, my name is, Cassie, and I help out here at Hedley Hall reading to the patients and writing letters for them. Is there someone you would like to send a message to? A worried mother perhaps?" she asked as she approached the cot.

Startled, turning his head toward her, he stuttered, "N-no, Ma'am. I don't want her to know about, well, about me."

"She must be worried since the government only sends notice that you have been seriously wounded, not anything else. A mother is bound to think the worse and worry that you need her help. Letting her know otherwise is really a way of telling her you care," explained Cassie.

"What can I say ta make her feel any better? That I'm blind and will never be nothin' but a burden ta her and Da? That's the reason I joined the infantry. Ta be somebody, ta take care of me self so they don't hafta worry 'bout feedin' me." His face was covered by the thick bandages Cassie was so used to seeing by now.

"Well, we can write that you are here and being taken care of medically. That you are well fed and recovering. That you are well enough to tell me what to write to her and to tell her you will be home in a few weeks," Cassie told him honestly.

The young man thought about it then said sheepishly, "Ma never learnt ta read. None of us can."

"That is not unusual, but is there a minister near your home? I can send the missive through him and he can take it to your mother and read it for her. He may even have time to send us back an answering note. I'm sure it would relieve her mind so much." Cassie urged the young man into taking interest in life again.

"I really don't know what ta say. I'm not the same boy that left her, ya know? Not jest 'cause I'm blind." Then he hung his head and almost whispered, "I think I went blind 'cause I saw so many bad things. It's my jest punishment. So much killin' and maimin', body parts scattered across a field where a few hours earlier we wuz all standing in our lines, ready ta take on the enemy, get the battle started and end the war. After a while, I think, we all jest wanted ta go home. On both sides, we wuz jest killing so that someone didn't kill us."

Cassie didn't interrupt his thoughts knowing that speaking about the horrendous tragedies seemed to cleanse the soldiers of their pain. And the guilt that while so many of their comrades died, they lived even though facing the future blind.

"I understand the soldier's dilemma. You went to fight for your country and you met up with young men like yourself who were there for the same reason. Only they were wearing a different color uniform. But that doesn't make you wrong or them right. Now we must focus on what you need, what will make you stronger and able to help your family when you return home. I can assure you that your mother wants you to return to her in any manner you can. This letter is the first and we needn't worry her about your sight right now. Let us let her know you are alive and are in good hands. I understand Dr. Landon is the best."

"Guess yer right, Ma'am. My Ma would want to hear from me now I'm back here in England. She said there was so much fever and such in Spain. She was sure I would catch it and die alone in a field." He sat up a little straighter on the cot.

"I know she would want to hear from you. Now where do you call home and where is the nearest church?" She glanced up to find Lord Hedley watching her with a stern expression in his eyes.

Cassie unobtrusively wiped the tears from her eyes and with an almost indistinguishable shake of her head let him know not to approach. She could handle the situation even if he felt her too soft. Lord Hedley stared at the ground then nodded to himself and walked on.

## CHAPTER THREE

In the quiet of her room, Cassie could finally think of herself and her personal feelings. She knew what she felt about helping the patients and Christopher, in particular. Although she was pleased with his potential recovery, he was still hesitant to go home and face Lucy or his mother. Otherwise, he had made great strides toward independence. In fact, all the men becoming independent regardless of their injuries were heading toward going home. Her work with them was bringing about the conclusion she wished for them. She knew it would take some longer than others to be ready to face their future at home.

Now Cassie was free to think about what or rather who she tried the hardest to ignore - Lord Headley. First, she thought he was someone she could mine for things she needed for the patients. As his generosity seemed to be endless and his criticism of anything she did nil, she began to look upon him as a man and not merely a host.

His attractiveness was impossible to ignore, at least for her in the confines of her room. She would close her eyes and see his smile, his dimples and the way a single eyebrow would rise in question or humor or interest. She was never sure which it was for certain.

And the way he moved. He would be standing quietly watching her with the men and then be next to her without her realizing he had moved. Moreover, it seemed he was always there at the most inopportune time. When she said something less than lady-like, or was touching a man's person even if such actions were due to her needing to help a patient.

And then there was that grin, that raised brow, that knowing look in his eye.

And the way her body reacted to his. It was like it knew when he was there watching her. Something would rush through her and she would know that when she glanced up, he would be there in the shadows watching, waiting, for what she didn't know.

She knew her body wanted to respond to his. She wanted to be nearer, smell him, touch him, taste him. She wanted her lips on his. On his body, taste him as she wanted him to taste her. These were the thoughts that would keep her awake some nights. Nights that she didn't understand the sensations rolling through her body, tightening the muscles low in her belly, making her writhe on the hot sheets.

In the morning, thankfully the feelings were less intense and she could almost forget she had ever felt them. That she had ever spent half the night thinking about a man who ignored her when she came too near. Other than being a good host, he seemed to want to remain at a distance. She needed to let the earl do that if she wished to help the men in the tents. She needed to stay focused on them and Christopher and getting all of them back home.

"Lord Hedley," called Cassandra from across the foyer before he could disappear down the hall to his library. He stopped and politely waited for her to continue. "I was hoping I could borrow Rex for the day."

Quinn asked, "Rex?"

"Yes, my lord, your dog. His name is Rex, I was told."

"I know the name of my own damn, er, my own dog. What surprises me is that you do and that you would wish to borrow him. I rarely let him roam free in the house." He explained, "He's young and has atrocious manners,"

"Well, I have to say they all do, my lord." She smiled sweetly up at him through her lashes which he knew boded ill for him and his belongings. "I wanted him to meet a couple of the men. Would that be all right?"

"Certainly, if that is your wish, Miss Woods. Try to see Rex doesn't knock any of the injured men down. He has a bad habit of jumping up on people, in a friendly way, but doesn't realize how big he is now."

"Thank you so much, my lord." The curtsey she gave him had more of smugness about it than he thought could be put into a curtsey.

Later in the afternoon, Quinn took a stroll toward the tents and saw Miss Woods surrounded by a small army of men, all in varying degrees of disrobement and dishevelment. Miss Woods seemed to be unaware of her associates' improper attire and held court as if in a private solon among the most sought-after poets and literary greats. They were debating a book they had finished reading and Miss Woods was first an opponent then a proponent of whichever side was losing.

"Lord Hedley, would you care to join us?" she asked loud enough for all to hear.

"No, I'm afraid I couldn't add anything to the discussion since I have not read the book in question," he answered. "Simply checking on whether you wanted me to take Rex back before he destroys something by chewing it to bits."

"Were you missing him?" she queried.

"No, I was missing a grandfather clock, but then I found it residing in the east wing," he said dryly.

"Well, yes. I knew you wouldn't mind. When one is without sight, it always seems like night. The chiming will help to keep one on a normal routine, my lord." Again, she wore that unfathomable smile. "As for Rex, I wouldn't wish to disturb him. He's resting beside Corporal Beals, newly arrived from the Peninsular, and they both need to stay quiet for a while."

At that, Beals swung his one leg over the edge of the bed with eyes staring blankly. Colorless eyes that Quinn still couldn't get used to. The young man said, "I much appreciated the use of your dog, m'lord. He reminds me of a setter I left at home. He was old when I left so I can't believe he'd be waitin' for me. It was good to feel a furry head again, I guess."

"Don't disturb yourself or Rex for me. I find him too distracting, always wanting to be played with or taken outside. It's best he stays here with you. Then I can get some work done," Quinn told the young man.

"We'll watch him for you, m'lord. No problem there." And the very young soldier unconsciously petted the now fawning dog next to him.

Quinn turned to Cassandra giving her a bow of a swordsman's acquiesce when he was bested. Still smiling, he returned to the house through the east wing, a clock chiming somewhere behind him.

How did this one young woman get so many men besotted so easily? Even his own staff cannot be trusted. That clock didn't move itself to the east wing though, to be fair, he had told Milton to give Miss Woods anything she required. It surprised him at the number and variety of items she felt necessary for the men's recuperation.

Not that he could fault her. Everything she has wanted or taken or confiscated has gone directly into use by or for the patients. She seems as interested in helping the lowliest recruit to the Major. Her betrothed had flourished under her care, appearing more like the young man he probably was when he bought his colors.

Everything he saw concerning that young lady showed her in the best light. Perhaps being brought here, to be confronted by how badly she had treated Moore, has turned her into a better woman. Someone worthy of being a wife to a man like Moore.

For some reason that thought did not sit well on his mind.


"What the hell do you think you're doing?" boomed a voice close behind her. She heard the patients begin to voice their outrage at having anyone speak to her so. Some stood up as if to go to her aid. She turned and looked at the man who voiced such displeasure.

"I was merely changing the bandage as per your instructions. Dr. Landon?" she asked.

Dr. Landon, a young man for such an esteemed doctor appeared to calm himself. "I'm sorry." He examined Christopher's hand, which had been badly burned when his rifle exploded. Picking it up, he studied the skin, then asked, "Do you have any more of this salve. It seems you have worked miracles on the burned skin in mere days. This appears as if it is barely going to scar."

"I have some, and I can make more. I know the recipe by heart," replied Cassie.

"You made it? Then it is a home remedy?" he asked

still looking at the burn.

"I'm a doctor of veterinary science and I first started making medicines for that purpose but I find they work as well on humans. After all, we are all God's creatures," she said still smiling and being accommodating so the doctor would not think she was trying to interfere with his patients.

The doctor returned her smile. "That we are. Carry on." And he walked to the next row of beds to consult with the patients there.

Cassie let out a big sigh and said cheerfully, "Now, where were we?"

Quinn wasn't surprised to see Cassandra at the center of a group of men at the edge of one of the tents. She had a soldier, missing his right leg and eyes staring blankly ahead, sitting in a chair with a towel wrapped around his shoulders. The young Mr. Beals if he remembered correctly. Cassandra, a comb in one hand and a deadly pair of scissors in the other, was cutting the young man's hair, talking all the while as she lifted and cut, lifted and cut. The men enraptured by every word.

"So, I have lots of practice cutting hair and you even stay still so I won't nip off a part of your ear or tail which is always a danger with my usual customers." Were the words Quinn heard when he arrived as the men laughed.

"Oh, Lord Hedley. My lord, we were talking about how difficult it is to recognize everyone from the sound of their footsteps. Some are very easy, like me since my skirts rustle and give me away, but others are more difficult, especially on the grass. I decided to try to announce myself prior to getting close enough to over-hear any conversation they may be having between themselves. Less chance for embarrassing explanations or apologies."

Several of the men nodded their heads in agreement even though only two of them there could actually see their consensus. Christopher Moore had the bandages off his eyes and although they were closed, he held his head up and smiled and laughed with the rest of the men. All the men were fully dressed, even their shoes were shined. It was a remarkable turnaround in a matter of a few days.

Quinn looked at Cassandra in a completely different light. She had earned all these men's trust in little less than a week and they showed more loyalty to her than they would to a commanding officer they may have been under for months. What was it about this young woman that seemed to draw males to her side? To make them want to be better than they were?

"I only have one more hair-cut to go. Then I was going to read more of the newspaper and perhaps start another novel. The men seem to have several favorites, but I don't have any of them with me, my lord," said Cassandra prettily smiling at him.

And had she actually fluttered her lashes? She was getting to be quite the minx. He would need to make sure he didn't get swept up in her trap as the other men seemed to be.

Plus, he was getting pretty certain when she called him 'my lord' it was actually something else she was saying.

Narrowing his eyes at Cassandra, Quinn tried to see an outline of a witch or demon overlaid on her profile, but there was none. Instead, he found himself offering to see what was available in the library that they may enjoy. He laughed at himself realizing he was being manipulated into doing as the Wiccan required.

Cassandra smiled prettily again. "Thank you, my lord."

Quinn gritted his teeth and left the group while trying to figure out what exactly Miss Woods was up to.

Cassie set a pattern for her day in the pavilion. She arrived early enough to help with setting out breakfast for what had become known as Cassie's troops. Then she read to the men, first the newspaper, kibitzing throughout the editorials and having loud discussions with the men about everything and anything. Making them defend their views. Making them think about the outside world. About what the rest of the world was doing.

Later she read the soldiers' private correspondence to them and wrote return letters as they were dictated. She also wrote to the families of men too wounded to think about home and family. Then there was luncheon and another reading session including the men's favorites and sometimes books of poems or sonnets she found in the Hedley library. Again, discussion was encouraged and the men argued over the political foundation of a poet's words or the interpretation of a sonnet's meaning.

In good weather, which was becoming more and more prevalent as spring went into summer, the afternoon walks with the men became longer and longer. New patients were indoctrinated into the 'system' the same as the originals had been, learning to navigate the stone paths, to walk with their heads upright and to make polite conversation. This was followed by tea usually in the garden or under one of the marquees if the weather were dreary.

In the evening, it became the habit for several of the soldiers to bring out their musical instruments to play for the others. It usually ended with a sing-a-long of folk and popular songs. The first time it occurred, a soldier who was blind and missing a leg from the knee down took out a well-loved violin and played a haunting melody.

There were tears streaming down his face as the music ended, but only Cassie was able to see and she would never tell anyone. "That was beautiful, Sergeant. Do you wish to play another?" The Sergeant took up the instrument again and played a jaunty country reel. Many of the men stamped their feet or tapped their hands to the music and all applauded when it was over. That first musical drew a soldier with a squeezebox and another with a flute. There was talent galore in these tents and Cassie seem to have brought it all to life.

One night as the Sergeant played a waltz, attended by the flute, the Major came over to Cassie and placed his cane against the chair. The Major was tall, dark hair clipped short and clean-shaven save for the mustache. Even with the black eyepatch he wore to cover the worse of the damage the shrapnel caused, he was devilish handsome. Cassie thought he knew it, too. Probably a rake prior to his service to crown and country. Definitely a man to watch if you had a marriageable daughter. He had always been the pillar of respectability with Cassie. He asked, "May I have the honor, Miss Cassie?"

Cassie smiled and stood up then curtseyed and replied, "Certainly. I have saved this dance for you on my card."

They stood facing one another and the Major placed his hand on Cassie's back and held his other hand out for Cassie to place her hand into then began the first step of the dance. It was amazing to Cassie the Major would take this chance and she was humbled he would feel safe enough with her to possibly stumble or even take a spill. Not that it would matter to her and perhaps that is what gave him the confidence to dance.

Cassie watched to make sure they weren't going to trip into anything. After all, they weren't on a cleared dance floor but in the grass at the edge of one of the tents. The Major twirled her expertly onto the grass and ended the dance with a bow as Cassie gave a curtsey.

"Thank you, Major, it's been years since I've waltzed, well, danced at all," Cassie admitted.

"Well, my dear, Miss Cassie, you haven't lost the touch. It was a pleasure to dance with you. We must do it more often," the Major said gallantly.

Cassie peered into the shadows of the house and saw Lord Hedley watching them, or her, intensely. He threw what must have been a lit cigar unto the path and it landed in an arc to die out harmlessly in the stones.

Cassie gave a little shiver. Somehow, she felt Lord Hedley's eyes were cold and accusing, but she couldn't be sure of his expression. Nonetheless, something about his stance made Cassie uneasy.

# CHAPTER FOUR

Quinn found Cassandra in the rose gardens with a scarf wrapped around her eyes. Actually, he had seen her from his library window and raced out needing to take this opportunity to speak with her alone for once. She was at a crossroads of the stone covered walkways between the bushes which were mulched and planted in tidy straight rows. The stone paths divided the sections to separate the different varieties of roses. Each section was marked by an engraved plaque telling the viewer the species and originality of the flowers they are viewing.

As Quinn drew near, he heard Cassandra yelp and put her finger quickly into her mouth.

"May I be of assistance, Miss Woods? I know these gardens well," he offered helpfully.

"I thought I did, too. It is so easy to get turned around. A short distance can seem like forever when you are trying to make your way in the dark."

"Exactly," he responded. "When Nathan was first home, he challenged me to 'walk in his shoes' so I did. I locked the library door and tried to walk from my desk to the sofa. A short space to navigate, but I kept veering off one way or the other, nearly tipping a lamp off a small stand. It could have started a dangerous fire if I hadn't opened my eyes when I hit my leg on the edge of the table. It was the beginning of my understanding of what Nathan was going through. Why it would seem so daunting to try to make a normal life out of what really is chaos."

Cassandra reached out her hand and met his arm. She gave it a pat as she turned toward the sound of splashing. "Oh, that must be the birdbath. I think I know where I am. I thought the fragrance of the different flowers would help me. That is what we concentrate on with the men, but the breeze can throw me off course and after a while all the flowers start to smell the same. It is a little off-putting. I know some of the men, like the Major, keep track of their steps or something. How he can do so and keep a proper conversation going is beyond me. He even does so while shortening his stride to walk beside me. Of course, he is very good at it."

Hearing her compliment another man on his ability seemed to make him grumpy but he shook it off. She was here and so was he.

"I am eager to oblige, Miss Woods. How much help do you wish from me?" Quinn asked as he watched her, the blindfold over her eyes doing strange things to him.

"Maybe a little hint. I am so tired of getting poked by the thorns."

"Two more steps, well three so your skirts don't catch, and you can turn either left or right. Does that help enough?"

"Perfectly, I know where I am in the garden now. I'll see if I can count steps to the next crossing."

"I'll walk with you, but I don't expect any polite chit-chat. Let's learn one thing at a time," he encouraged.

Quinn was prepared to remain quiet, but for Cassandra that was impossible. Her mind was always going, always investigating, learning new things, probing and prodding to get to the facts then analyzing them until she was satisfied, until she understood it all. He should have been prepared to be pumped for information or favors.

"Lord Hedley, I was speaking to Lady Melanie this morning and she thinks you had a great deal of responsibility for her husband's change of mind about his blindness. Did you do something that brought your brother back from despair? Was there something that works for the newly blinded?"

"I don't wish to speak of it. It was a private matter between my brother and me," Quinn told her dismissively.

"But if it would help me find a way in, to give these men hope when they are hopeless. Could you not share that even if it is embarrassing to you or your brother? You know I do not judge, but Lady Melanie is so pleased with her relationship with Colonel Lancaster, with his altered state of mind. I wondered if it would work with the other men who have not accepted their blindness, yet."

"I took a great chance. I don't know if you would dare try it with a soldier you did not know well," he said hesitantly. Miss Woods didn't know what she asked of him. In a way, he was a little ashamed of what he had put his brother through, the walking on coals to bring him back to them, him and Melanie. He thanked God it worked and he wasn't sure there were two miracles in the same method.

Quinn stopped, bowing his head, almost in prayer and quietly told Cassandra what he had done. Like a priest, her eyes covered, head bent towards the confessor to hear the softly spoken words.

"I fought with him." The words quiet in the otherwise normal day. "I wanted to get him so mad he would fight me. When I found my gun missing…." He paused remembering the rush of fear that almost numbed him, then continued, "I checked it daily and thought he couldn't find it, but he did. I knew where he would go. Out of the house, out into the fields to the woods so that when he was found it wouldn't be by a family member. I ran after him, following the trail he left trying to feel his way to the woods. It felt unfair the blindness that made him want to commit suicide was the same blindness that allowed me to follow the path to his chosen site.

"I confronted him. I accused him of being a coward for not fighting for a life. I accused him of not loving Melanie. I accused him of being selfish by being submerged in his own pity. He lunged at me, he tried to hit out at me. Some of the time the fists struck home and some of the time I let them. I don't know how long we fought, but after a while we were both so tired, we were merely swinging at air. Swearing at each other, damning each other."

He remembered the moment as if it were yesterday. "Finally, when we were too tired to fight any longer, I offered to shoot him myself if that is truly what he wanted. If the loss of his sight outweighed the gain of his life. If Melanie and myself were not enough reason to go on, if the possibility of having a son and daughter was not reason enough to go on, then I would help him let go."

With a little lighter voice, he continued, "However, I pointed out that any son-of-a-bitch who fought so hard, and possibly broke one of my teeth, probably didn't really want to end his life. It shouldn't be so hard to kill a man who really wanted to die."

Cassandra was quiet for a moment. "You were very

brave to confront Colonel Lancaster in that manner. The demons could have won out and then what? But you are right. I couldn't use the same method. You must really love your brother. You are a good man, Lord Hedley."

Cassie felt Quinn turn her towards him and place a kiss lightly on her lips. Her breath caught in her throat as she felt his lips on hers. She heard him turn on the stones and listened to the sound of his footsteps as they faded leading back toward the manor. Cassie's tears for the pain she knew both he and Colonel Lancaster went through slid from under the blindfold.

She waited a moment for his departure not wishing to embarrass either of them. She couldn't handle what she was feeling. Not now. Not when so many needed her. Wiping away her tears, she gained her composure. Unsure her experiment in the garden was a success, she removed the blindfold and headed toward the front of the house.

"Milton," Cassie called out to get the butler's attention before he disappeared into the lower sanctum of the house. "The men and I were discussing things they would like to do, things they may have been doing today if they hadn't lost their sight. I was wondering if there were any fishing poles or gear about?"

"Fishing poles, Miss?" asked the butler as only a trained butler could ask.

"Yes, fly-fishing to be precise. Lieutenant Moore was quite good, I know, and he can swim if he slips in, but I'll go with them. I can cast pretty well and we will have to figure out all the complications of fishing without sight. Oh, and are there any bow and arrows. You know, to set up an archery range just past the pavilion," continued Cassie. She was getting more and more enthusiastic about the idea of giving the men some challenges to keep them from becoming bored or fretting over what their lives will be like once they are healed.

"I'll see what there is, Miss. One of the footmen will let you know." He gave a slight bow.

"Oh, thank you, Milton, the men will be so appreciative." Cassie turned smiling and returned to the tents.

Milton was true to his word. Within a matter of hours there were several poles, waders and an assortment of fishing flies in a wicker box delivered to the tent. The bow and arrows had seen better days, but with a little restringing, they too were ready for use. Now she needed to figure out what to shoot at without endangering anyone.

Lord Hedley sauntered by and caught Cassie's eye. She glanced up hoping he was willing to return to their usual manner with one another. "My Lord, have you come to participate in our lawn party?"

"I heard something about some outside activities progressing. Are you prepared for all the excitement?" Cassie realized he was warning her about possible complications.

"We have men who are interested in both the fishing and archery. I am competent in both sports so am prepared to personally help with anything they might find difficult. I was going to attend both activities since one will be in the early morning while the other can be done anytime during the day, well, actually night too since it doesn't matter to the men," Cassie said without indication of either humor or pity.

"I have a gamekeeper, his job is more in husbandry than watching for poachers, but he enjoys early morning fishing along the river. He often brings brook trout for Cook. I may send a sturdy footman, too, in case someone needs to be rescued. He'll be discreet as to his reason for being with them."

She recognized the offer for what it was, protection for the men.

"That would be wonderful. The men can use the exercise. They say they are getting too fat and happy having everything done for them. They are used to doing more physical activities and are finding the sitting around recovering a little boring," Cassie explained, as Lord Hedley seemed not to be in a hurry.

"Well, I don't know how you plan to get them to hit anywhere near a target, but I am having the one I used to use at house parties taken down from the attic of the barn. It has a straw back with a canvas painted target. The rest is up to you."

"Thank you. That is more than generous of you, my lord," said Cassie as she smiled her Mona Lisa smile.

Quinn turned to walk back to the house when he stopped, turned, and asked, "Did I actually see two patients playing checkers?"

"Yes, I marked the reds with a little cross cut into the top and the blacks are left as is. I scribed into the board the boundaries of each square and put an X on those that should be red. There's been a slight discussion about cheating. One man was sure another moved a checker, but I told them both to listen. That they could hear an opponent move any checker and keep them honest by knowing every move made. I explained they should picture the board and every square in their mind and they will know if a checker is out of place because they can replay the entire game if need be."

"Do you think that will work?" he asked concerned.

"Both the Major and Christopher have been playing chess that way. They even take breaks and can restart a game if they get interrupted. I have played with Christopher, using a board and pieces, but he still gets the best of me. Always did."

By late afternoon, the target was set-up in place and the equipment ready for use. Cassie stood several yards from the painted canvas circle and knocked the arrow. Pulling the string back and up in the same smooth motion, she let the string go as the arrow became perpendicular with the target. A bull's eye. Cassie squealed with delight. The sighted footmen's mouths fell open, but snapped shut quickly.

"Now, gentlemen," she addressed the waiting participants. "I made a bull's eye, just as I will every time I take a shot at the target, whether I actually do or not. As gentlemen, you will applaud my accomplishment and as a lady, I will make my curtsey to you in return." Cassie teased the men, hoping they will accept their limitations with humor.

The men laughed, as she wanted them to and some of the tension she felt surrounding them lessened. To many, this was more than a game. This was a test for them to see if they could perform any of their former tasks, if they could go home and pick-up any part of their old lives.

"All right Christopher, I'll start with you since I know you have experience. I'll stand right behind you and point you toward the target. Now I have placed a sound maker, a little windmill, on top of the straw. It is about two feet higher than the bull's eye. Now knock your arrow and pull your string back, take aim and let the arrow go when you're ready. If you miss, I have a couple of footmen fleet of, er, of foot, to retrieve the arrows that miss their mark. I expect they will get more of a work-out than any of us." Cassie glanced over to the footmen to see them trying to hide their smiles.

Christopher knocked the arrow, pulled back on the string and held the arrow almost perpendicular. Cassie reached around him, telling him she was doing so, and lifted the arrow a little, saying, "Listen to the ticking of the windmill. Sense where it is and aim a little lower."

Christopher let the string go smoothly and the arrow hit the straw just off the painted target.

"Very good. It hit to the right, about two o'clock, and up about half a yard. Possibly I shouldn't have helped by raising your arrow point. This time I'll stay out of it. It's all you, boyo," she teased.

Christopher did the same things he did the first time, but took into consideration the over-shot and tried to compensate. This time the arrow hit the target.

Cassie said, "A little right of the bull's eye and I stayed away from helping you. One more arrow and we'll give another a try at it. I don't want you over-working that shoulder, after all you recently got out of a sling. Dr. Landon will have my head if I let you pull a tendon and set your recovery back. Now who is to be next?"

The Major, his military uniform pristine stepped forward with a regal bearing and held out his hand for the bow. One eye was covered by a silk eyepatch and the other stared blankly, the once blue center a milky-white. Cassie placed the weapon into his hand and the process began.

After the shot, which went high and wide, Cassie diplomatically said, "Well, Major, you will win the competition on distance. You probably could use a heavier bow for target shooting, but a stag on the run wouldn't have a chance against your arrow. Now let me stand behind you to help lower the arrow to be perpendicular to the bull's eye."

The lesson continued until all the men who had an interest went through the routine three times, each time showing a little improvement and a little more confidence when holding the equipment. Cassie was pleased as she noted the difference this simple activity brought about in the men.

She began to rack her brain to include more of these same types of activities. She needed to give each of the men here a chance to recover some of what he lost along with his eyesight.

Early the next morning a footman came in to the breakfast room to tell Cassie that Christopher and two others were ready to go fly-fishing. She gulped down her tea and quickly excused herself.

Cassie came running down the front steps and asked the footman who was going to accompany them, "Which way to the river?" Then she followed his lead. She took Christopher's arm and made sure the others walked next to a sighted person to help negotiate the way.

"I've noted the morning sun feels warmer on my face when I head north or south, but almost not at all going west. It probably is the opposite in the late afternoon," she said to no one in particular.

Christopher asked teasingly, "Is this going to turn into an experiment, Cassie? Should I be afraid you're going to push me into the stream so you can decide whether I can make my way back to the river bank without aid?"

"Now Christopher," she chided, "Have I ever done that to you before?"

"You mean like when I was twelve and you talked me into going into the stream holding a rock and then ever bigger rocks until I could no longer stay above water? Just so you could study the ratio of effort to stay floating to the amount of dead weight it would take to drown me?"

"That wasn't the hypothesis at all and you know it. I was trying to determine how much dead weight a healthy swimmer can lift, such as an unconscious swimmer, and bring them both to safety at the river's bank. Completely worthwhile and I would have mourned for weeks if it had ended any other way." She tucked her arm through Christopher's and hugged him to her.

Quinn stayed behind the group, but close enough to hear Cassandra and Christopher who were taking up the rear. He watched as Cassandra kept an eye out for anything that may trip up the non-sighted men in the group as well as keeping up unending chatter. If she wanted the men to know where she was, she was doing a good job of it.

Uncharacteristically pulling a frown, he thought if he had his damn dog, he would have been out walking it instead of following behind this group. Watching Moore make a fool of himself over the woman who betrayed him while he was off fighting in the war made something deep in his stomach tighten.

Didn't the man realize Miss Woods paid almost as much attention to every other young man? Hell, even the older men weren't passed by. The woman must have self-assurance a mile wide to think all these men should pay her court. Quinn wasn't fooled by a pretty face and enchanting smile. He knew her true worth and one day he would see to her comeuppance.

Earlier in the week, she asked to be excused from most of the meals so she could eat with the men. Melanie thought it was romantic Cassandra could not pull herself away from Lieutenant Moore even to eat inside, but Quinn thought Cassandra was being foolish. It wasn't as if anyone could see her there eating with the men. Besides he liked having her at table telling him what she and the men were doing, how her plans were progressing, how Lieutenant Moore was progressing, and if he were healed enough to go home soon.

Quinn huffed out a discontented sigh. Why was it he found himself thinking about this woman? This one woman who clearly belonged to a blinded veteran. He didn't wish to examine his feelings too closely. He had already convinced himself the kiss in the garden was due to the emotion surrounding the topic they had been discussing. She had been the only person he had told about finding Nathan near the wood. The only person he felt close enough to tell. He trusted she would be discreet and keep his confidence. That she also sensed how it made him feel was what brought about the kiss. Nothing more. There could never be more. He knew what was right and he would follow the dictates of his station and position. Miss Woods was under his care while at the manor and she was still the affianced of Lieutenant Moore. And Quinn better remember it.

The party reached a clearing near the edge of the stream. Cassie nodded her approval to the gamekeeper.

There were no low hanging branches within range of the fishermen and the stream moved at a healthy speed, but not one that would cause alarm. The sandy bottom showed some shallows and large stones dotted along the stream with others holding the bank in place.

The three couples, a sighted with the non-sighted and Quinn standing back until he was needed, spaced themselves along the stream so that each had room to maneuver. The men wore waders and entered the water slowly. They had all practiced casting on the open front lawn at the manor, but now when faced with reality, Christopher froze.

Cassie stood close so she could encourage him without the others ascertaining his fear. "I will describe the stream exactly. It doesn't seem much different than the Worther back home. We knew that stream blindfolded and now you will get to know this one the same way. Hold my waist and I will walk down to the water's edge. It has no bushes and the bottom is clear for about four-feet out. Not a fast stream, but there is a current running about a foot under the water's surface." She led Christopher into the water, her skirts drawn between her legs and floating downstream with the current. "Do you have your footing? I won't leave you."

Cassie saw Lord Hedley standing near the edge of the stream a few yards away from the couples. He seemed worried for her. Probably thought the weight of her wet skirts would make her unsteady and fall in to get borne downstream, unable to get to the shore or grab onto anything. She wanted to assure him she was safe, but her main attention was on Christopher.

Continuing to speak quietly to Christopher, he was soon standing straight and began the soothing movement of flicking the pole, hearing the fly move through the air and land with a soft kerplunk followed by a slight sound of the line being pulled with the current. Reeling in the line and holding it, he then repeated the movement.

Eventually, Cassie said quietly, "Is it as you remember?"

"Sh-h-h, there's a fish trying to take the fly. My God, I can feel every nibble. I'm like one with the pole. This is fantastic, Cassie," he whispered.

Then he snapped the pole tip up and set the hook. Christopher played the fish like a dancing partner. Eventually the fish tired and Christopher brought the fish in with Cassie helping by grabbing it as it broke surface.

"How big is it? It felt like a monster," he asked excitedly.

"About a foot long, I'd guess," Cassie said as excitedly.

"Oh, that won't be more than a couple of bites. Throw it back and let it grow a little bit more." He laughed as he let Cassie remove the fly and lower the fish into the water to swim into the shadows.

A few hours later the little group travelled back to the manor, wet, a little fishy and yet as grand as conquering heroes. Each of the blind soldiers had caught at least one fish, mostly trout, and no one had taken a dunking. Something Cassie was thankful for.

Christopher walked beside her, quietly thinking before saying, "I'm going home aren't I, Cassie? I owe it all to you. You know, I love you." He pulled her arm through his and matched her steps.

Quinn, bringing up the rear again, pursed his mouth and Cassie thought she heard him say under his breath, "What a lucky bastard."

# CHAPTER FIVE

The next morning, the talk was still about the fish and as with most fish stories, the caught fish kept getting longer and longer. Finally, Cassie warned all the fishermen if they kept telling tales their audience would require the fish so they could verify the size.

After that, there was only talk about how big the next fish were going to be. Now that the men proved they could fly-cast, they wanted to return to the river in other areas even if it meant getting the fly tangled in over-hanging branches occasionally. Something that had happened even when they had their sight.

Some of the men who never fished before asked questions about how it was done and if it must be fly-fishing only. Some of the more experienced fishermen assured them that dropping a line off the side of the bridge was a satisfying manner of fishing, as well, and the fish tasted just as good.

Cassie decided it was time to talk basic public skills. The group was the usual one to surround her, the men who were original bunkmates around Christopher's bed with a couple of additions like the Sergeant and the Major who both slept inside the east wing of the manner. The latter man having both a valet and more personal comforts than the others.

"Being blind makes traveling, whether across the tent or across a dance floor, a tenuous trip. I have noticed that it causes some of you to tip your head up or hang your head to your chest. Either is disconcerting to those around who are sighted. I will help you regain a natural pose while sitting or standing, but it may require me to touch your person. Please permit me to help you with this. If my touch bother's you, let me know. I will honor your wishes."

There were murmurs of agreement to her help.

"The next housekeeping is a little disconcerting for me, but it is something I feel is as important as any other. Many of you have gotten used to putting your hands out in front of you, keeping yourselves from banging your face into anything although it doesn't save your shins."

Several men laughed and nodded their heads in agreement.

"I am used to those actions and have successfully stayed out of reach. Women in the outside world will not be as aware of your actions. I would rather none of you get beat with an umbrella, which believe me is what a governess carries an umbrella for, when you unfortunately place your hands upon some lady's person in error."

There was some laughter at that and many asked what else could they do?

"If I may use you as an example, Major?"

"Certainly, Miss Cassie, I am always at your disposal," he answered politely.

"The Major carries a very stylish cane. He keeps it on his right side and leads with his right foot when beginning any movement. Before he starts out, he places the cane ahead of his body and can feel if the ground remains flat or not. If there is something the cane hits he can stop and discern, with a little cane movement, whether it is something that will trip him. If so, he veers away from it." Turning towards the Major she asked,

"Are there any other secrets to you being able to travel so well unassisted?"

"I did not realize you were so aware of my, um, traveling, Miss Cassie. But no, you seem to have caught all my secrets with the cane," he replied.

The men dispersed, each with their own ideas as to what type of cane to get or how to keep out of trouble with the males of women they may come in contact with.

The Major came forward, standing straight in his uniform and polished boots, and bowed toward Cassie. "May I have the honor of introducing you to my mount, Triumph? He is a particularly fine example of English horse flesh."

Cassie glanced enquiringly at the Major and decided the invitation wasn't a euphemism and answered, "I would love to see the horse that made it through so many campaigns without a mark." She stood and took the arm the Major winged out.

The two strolled across the grass and onto the gravel drive that fronted the house.

"I hope I didn't disconcert you with my lesson of today," Cassie said. "I apologize if I went too far. My father used to complain I was too outspoken for a refined female, which only went to prove what I had been telling him from the time I was out of leading strings. Not that I think my nurse ever could keep me in leading strings. I should have been born a boy. Then my father would have gotten his heir and I would have had the freedom to be me from a younger age."

"My dear lady, don't say such things. You are a breath of fresh air in an otherwise dismal world. I find I wake up each morning eager to find out what you will get us into next. I have been surprised from the first morning that I happened to hear you tell a story about a three- legged dog and naming him Lucky." He smiled at the memory.

"Actually, Lord Hedley thought that would be a good name for him. I unimaginatively named him Bertram after a boy I used to know." She hesitated, then continued, "Oh dear, I should not repeat this, I'm sure, but I named the dog that because along with losing a hind leg I, umm, removed his, I mean, he needed to be castrated. I did not care for this Bertram ergo the poor dog became his namesake." Cassie giggled and the Major laughed outright, big gusts of laughter.

"Remind me if I ever get on the wrong side of you, Miss Cassie. I do wish to keep the body parts I have left. Oh, damn! Pardon my language, but I have lost track of my count."

"Your count, Major? May I help?" she offered confused.

"Yes, it is the least you can do since my worry over my body parts caused the whole thing. I keep track of the number of steps. Twenty-seven steps between the ends of the tents and the beginning of the drive, stay on the gravel two hundred and thirty-five steps, which will bring me to the stables, but of course, I can smell it before I need to keep count. The whole idea is to know how many steps are between any two points and I can travel easily wherever I want within my own world," he explained.

"Well, we are about fifty steps to the edge of the drive and you should be able to start your count again," Cassie encouraged.

"Thank you, Miss Cassie. I can handle it from here." He gave a small bow.

The major was right in saying the stables were redolent of horse and hay and grain. Not smells that affronted Cassie, of course being a veterinarian, and ones she found she missed not working with the animals she so loved.

But these men were more important and their time of need more immediate. As they entered the stable, Cassie knew instantly which horse belonged to the Major. She went up to the horse that must be Triumph and began rubbing the soft nose including rubbing into its nostrils. She began the cooing that women used with babies and animals, telling him how beautiful he is, how big and strong, how brave he is to have gone into battle after battle.

Major Bradley stood beside Cassie as she talked quietly with the large horse. A horse she felt he owed his life to for getting him through so many battles and home again. He seemed bemused standing there while a woman complimented his horse on its strong fetlocks and silky tail.

On the return trip to the pavilion, Cassie asked. "What are your plans for Triumph after you leave here?"

"I will take him back to my country manor and put him out to stud. I have a couple of mares that I will probably breed first. He has excellent blood lines." Then he seemed to recall to whom he was speaking and said, "Oh, I beg your pardon. Not exactly parlor talk. Well, that's brought about a blush. Something I haven't done since leaving home for school."

"Please, Major. I am a veterinarian and I miss talking shop, as one might say. I think that is an excellent idea, but why put him out to pasture?"

"What are you saying, Miss Cassie? I shouldn't put

him out to stud?"

"I think you should put him out to stud, but you could keep riding him, as well."

The Major stopped walking and became very still, excitement seeming to race through him. Then he shook his head evidently tamping down the thought of such independence being his again. "I haven't ridden since my injuries. I don't think it's possible. Being led around the paddock by a stable boy like a child on his first pony? No, I don't think that would be for me."

"I don't think it would be that way at all. After all, I've seen a blind horse pull a wagon on a milk route. He never missed a stop."

"Are you comparing me with a milk horse?" He sounded both affronted and entertained.

She patted his arm to sooth his injured ego. "I think Triumph is an intelligent animal and wouldn't let you get into harm's way. You have told us stories of how he saved you over and over during a battle, facing cannon fire, standing between you and danger. I think your horse will be more than competent to have you ride out on him. A groom would need to go along, or someone else you trust, but I don't think riding is an impossibility for the blind."

The Major was quiet on their walk back toward the tent then he excused himself for his preoccupation. "I'm sorry for being such a poor companion. It is simply the chance of having the freedom to mount a horse again. The feel of the wind as we race over an open field is like giving a starving man food. I want it so badly I can almost feel the horse beneath me, sailing over a hedge, thundering hooves in the morning dew covered grass. Because I love it so much and a horse needs his master, not be put out to pasture. Perhaps I should at least try. Take a chance to enjoy life as I use to."

They stopped at the tents and joined the ever-growing members of Cassie's troop. She hoped this would be one of many walks and talks between the Major and herself. His limp was mostly hidden, only indicated when he bent down and needed to keep that leg stiffened. He should be able to travel quite a distance before it effected his knee. Riding again would be most beneficial to the officer, Cassie was sure of it. She was so glad she had taken this walk with him.

Staring into the empty fireplace of the library, Quinn wondered if getting a servant to light a fire would warm his soul. Chase the chill he felt whenever he was alone. But why was he so despondent? His brother's sight was returning, slowly, but Nathan said he is seeing more and more daily. His sister-in-law is the happiest he'd seen her since before Nathan went to war. The troops seemed to be more organized and even he could see the improvement in their lives and attitudes. Ever since Cassie…. Was that the root of both changes? His melancholy and the others' good humor?

"Lord Hedley, may I have a moment of your time?"

Think of the devil and he shall appear. "You may have as much of my time as you need, Miss Woods. I'm here for the evening." He couldn't help but smile since he knew she would have continued with asking what she needed of him either way. He had figured out her way of manipulating people into doing what she wished them to do. Why fight it?

Sipping from the dark amber liquid in the glass, he

caught her watching him closely. "May I have one of those?"

Holding up the partially filled glass, his brows rose in question. "One of these? It's whiskey, you know."

"Yes, please, my lord. I was hoping it was." Then stood expectantly as he poured two-fingers into an empty glass next to the decanters. Handing it to her, she sipped and sighed. "It's been a while but nothing tastes like *ulsge-beatha*, the water of life."

He was impressed she hadn't collapsed in a coughing fit due to the strength of the drink but demurred to say anything so unkind.

Sitting crosswise in the chair, with her legs over the arm made her appear as a young girl, one shoe hanging off her stockinged toes with each swing of her foot. He wondered if that were the first strong liquor she had ever drank then thought better of it. He sat so they were on the same plane.

"I take it that isn't the first glass of whiskey you've ever consumed?" His smile tinged his words. He couldn't help that being with her made him feel happy. And the emotion was at contrast with how he had felt moments before she arrived. He would think on that another time. Now he merely wanted to hear her speak.

"Um, a hanging-on from my misspent youth, I'm afraid," she teased taking another swallow.

"Misspent youth?"

"Well, to be truthful it was during my university days. While I was taking classes to become a veterinarian. My aunt pulled all sorts of strings to get me accepted but there were those who opposed a woman learning anything more than deportment and how to dance. Said I would be a distraction to the other students who would use their education wisely." She pulled a face which made him smile again. "As if I were there on a lark."

"I can see where someone as lovely as you would be a distraction to young men of a certain age."

"Oh, not you, too, my lord. I had plenty of that in my time. Men who thought that if one wasn't a plain-faced, long-legged Nell then she must not have a brain. I can tell you now that I passed my exams with flying colors. Difficult since I took the course in about half the time the others took it. I didn't want to waste time in class. I wanted to use my knowledge."

"So, the other students accepted you being there? No problems, I take it?"

"Oh, no problems once I was outfitted as the male student I would be known as."

He sputtered, spewing his drink as he did so over the front of his shirt. Gazing at her amazed, he needed her to repeat her words. "You what?"

"I dressed as any of the other students. Even had a mustache to detract from my female profile." She laughed. "That got me into trouble more than once."

Still smiling at his mental image of what she must have looked like as a boy, he asked, "How so?"

"We were all out at a pub…."

"Wait. You were drinking in a pub? With the other students?"

"Yes, of course. I needed to blend in with them so I needed to do as they did out of class as well as in it. Otherwise I would have drawn too much attention to myself."

He urged her back to her story. "So, you and your school mates were in a pub and…."

"And we were drinking this rubbish of a port. We had each pitched in and bought a pitcher of the stuff. It was bitter and smelled of skunk. I do not lie. It was awful but none of us would say so because none of us knew what it should have tasted like."

"What were the ages of these other students?"

"You must remember, my lord, that we are not speaking of a group of hell-raisers. These were young men wanting to have a career in caring for farm livestock and possibly making their families' lives better breeding stronger, meatier animals."

"Point taken. Go on."

"Well, we were swilling it down and I kept wiping my mustache because I didn't want it dripping on my waistcoat when all of a sudden, everyone stopped joking and talking and stared at me. Right at my mouth." This part seemed to have tickled her since she giggled again placing her hand over her mouth a little too late. "I, ah," Giggle. "I, I." Giggle. "I had wiped my mouth so often I had disturbed my mustache to the point it was hanging from one side of my lip."

He laughed picturing her sitting there in public exposed as the female she was. "What happened? Did they tell anyone?"

"They told everyone who would listen once they were back in class." Sobering up a little she continued, "I, on the other hand, had to admit I couldn't grow a mustache but wanted to appear older to a certain young lady I cared about so paid for the mustache made of horse hair. I said once I had appeared in the dratted thing, I had to keep doing so or people would wonder…."

Still smiling she confessed, "I had more than one student ask me where I got the thing since they, too, told me they couldn't grow a decent face of hair. I told them and they all began to sprout mustaches, goatees and even a Vandyke."

Quinn found the story hilarious but merely laughed wondering at how the group he ran with at university would have handled the situation. Probably pretty much the same although they might have put the lad up to even more ridicule. Perhaps these boys were softer hearted than most English students when it came to being fallible.

The silence nagged at him. He wanted to hear more about her. Anything at all. "Tell me more about your university days."

"Oh, no. I'm not playing that game. I invented that game."

"What game is that?" He couldn't help smiling. She appeared so charming, so entertaining he had almost forgotten why she was in that chair.

"The game where you tell someone something about yourself that you had never told another soul." She took a drink and giggled. "When it got to be my turn, I confessed I was a virgin."

"You didn't?" Aghast a young woman would have said such a thing in public, no less. "To a pub full of young men? How did they respond? What did they say?"

"Well, I was speaking as one male to another.… Most of them admitted they were also and wanted to get rid of that particular burden before returning to their home towns. It ended with us making a pledge to find a bawdy house and rid ourselves of the curse of childhood and become men."

Sitting almost dumbstruck he squeaked, his voice rising higher with each word, "How did you get out of that?"

Shrugging, she drained the glass and held it out to him waggling it. He stood and filled it again without thinking. Focusing on the information she had pledged to rid herself of the burdensome virginity. Sitting hard as the strength in his legs failed him, he watched her take another swallow wondering what the polite way of asking her if she were still a virgin. The answer may free up a worry he had had about her since her arrival to his home.

"I went with them once we found the right place. The Knight's Club just off the main road from the campus. It was lovely inside and out. Quiet the proper place for such things."

"Do not tell me you entered? Tell me you told everyone you had become ill or some such…."

"What? And have all of them think I couldn't go through with it? No, I did as the others. I dressed in my best clothes, combed my hair – and mustache – and walked the mile or so to the door. Once inside, we were met by a gallery of women. All sizes, ages and colors. Well, you must know." She said with a wave of her hand while he thought about denying ever being within the walls of a bawdy house or anything resembling one. He gave up on that idea almost as soon as it entered his head.

"Most of us were in awe, and the women all knew why we were there so were patient and kind as we finally found our way through the picking out of our companions."

He had his face buried in his hands, shaking his head but remaining quiet. Not allowing the groans of mortification to escape although it was becoming more and more difficult to do so. Cassie seemed lost in memories which didn't seem sad or embarrassing for her.

"The others left one by one with the younger women but I selected an older woman, Collett Versailles, teasing the rest with the information that my father had given me the hint that experience would pay for itself in those kind of places."

The moan escaped his lips and he pressed them tighter together but couldn't wait to hear what had happened. He felt a voyeur in her life needing to hear of her experiments, her knowledge.

"She took me upstairs and asked me what I thought I would like from her." He dared stare over at Cassie and found a half-smile on her lips. "I explained that I was a virgin and wanted to know what it would be like to be with a man."

"Oh, my God. You are part devil, I swear." He found the words blurting from his mouth. His fingers dug into his hair as he imagined the expression on the harlot's face.

"No, I figured she had guessed my secret long before I revealed it. Remember, this was her work. She had had plenty of young boys from the school and elsewhere in that place."

"And what did she say?"

"I asked and she answered. Then we simply sat around for a while talking about men in general. Her life and how she had ended up there. She gave me good answers. Some very similar to the ones my aunt had passed on to me."

Another groan. He didn't need to hear all of this. He wanted to but he didn't need to.

"Have I ever explained my aunt's feeling on being

female?" At the shake of his head, she continued, "Aunt Laura thinks that males may have the muscles but it is the female that is the strongest. Look at the wars and countries when led by males and look at them when females are at the head. Cleopatra took down the Roman Empire after hundreds of years of having men try do so. Men fail so often due to their innate weakness – which are females. We can get men to do anything we want given the right motivation. We bear the next generation, raise it and give it it's base of thinking. We can persuade them to go one way or the other. Presently, men think because they go to university and hold the titles, they hold the power. But look at all the men taken down from both of those and you'll find a woman behind it."

He had to admit she had some good points – or perhaps it was only the whiskey thinking so. The mantel clock striking midnight seemed to being them both back to the library where they had been holed up for hours.

"Oh, look at the time. I must go to bed or will be too tired for our trek tomorrow. Some of the men have decided to try to walk further afield and to see if they can make it back without issue." She rose gracefully, all signs of the hoyden lounging in his chair earlier, gone.

"Ah, yes, yes, of course." He hated this night to end even if some of it were almost painful mentally to live through. Her stories only wetted his appetite for more. How did she live in the dormitory surrounded by all those boys? How did she keep her lovely long hair hidden? How did she buy clothes that fit?

Quinn searched around his bedroom and asked himself, *what did I come up here for?'* but found himself watching out over the front lawn and drive. That was why he was really up there. He searched the green grass and the tan gravel and there, standing next to the Major, was Cassie. He inhaled deeply watching as the couple stood and had what seemed to him, a serious discussion for several minutes. Quinn wished he was as easy going as Cassie's troops seemed to be with her. Every time Quinn and Cassie were together, he felt he must hold back, hide something, although he wasn't sure what. He had never known feelings like this for a woman.

This something, this hidden something that could not be named. He wasn't sure what to do about it, but he knew he was getting less and less able to hold it in check. The other day he sat up here for hours in this window and watched the men practice fly casting. Watched as Cassie went from one man to another on the front lawn like a butterfly to flowers. Placing her hands on theirs, standing close enough for their bodies to have been touching, pressing her breasts to their backs, their sides.

In reality, she probably hadn't touched them, never in that way, but to him, from there, that was all he could think about. How he would exchange places with them so that she touched him in such a personal manner. He ached with the need to have her all to himself.

He found it excruciating to sit there and watch while feeling left out of her realm. Yet he lacked the strength of will to turn away, to return to the library. Quinn knew he needed to overcome this infatuation or attraction or whatever it was. He should turn away and leave now, but he continued to watch until his target was out of view for several minutes.

Hissing out a breath, he became angry at himself for not having the strength to turn away, ignore the damn woman or tell her to go home. She had caused enough upset among the men.

While at the same time, he feared hearing the doctor tell him that all the men are better or as healed as they can be and should be sent home. Cassie would be sent home, too. Possibly, no probably, to marry Lieutenant Moore. To make love with that man and to bear his children.

Quinn slapped his own leg in frustration he couldn't control. He must stop thinking of her as anything but Lieutenant Moore's fiancée and a helpmate for the doctor. He must get her out of his house but first he must get her out of his mind.

Entering the room knowing he had seen her gown disappear down the hallway towards the library, Quinn asked, "Looking for more books, Miss Woods?"

"Just something boring to put me to sleep, my lord. The ones I select to read with the men are more challenging. I need to keep on my toes or lose an argument to one of them." Her hands fluttered over a small book of poems then moved on.

"I could share my decanter of whiskey with you." He continued walking on to the small credenza holding the beverages and tumblers. Lifting up the decanter, his brows rose in query.

"Why not? I slept very soundly last time." She strolled over and accepted the glass of amber liquid before taking her place in her chair. He would forever think of that particular chair as hers. He had given up trying not to do so.

He was glad she had brought the last time up since the questions had been keeping him awake. That night as well as many others. He couldn't stop imagining her in his first-year dormitory at Cambridge. "I was wondering what Madam Collett and you spoke about while you spent time together. It must have been very informative for a virgin, for any eighteen-year old girl." He surprised himself at his rashness in speaking the truth. But somehow, during all those nights he imagined Cassie and him together he had become much more intimate in his thinking of her. As if they had known one another longer and closer than in actuality.

"Yes, I learned about the male in general. How they think and act when no one else is there to admonish or censure. I also learned they are much more vulnerable than anyone would guess. I think what I learned that night has helped me with the troops."

His shocked gasp escaped after promising himself she would no longer be able to surprise him.

"I mean, that men were just as sensitive to rejection, to feeling needed, being wanted as females are. We are not that much different from one another all in all." She sipped and watched him as if expecting an argument.

He didn't have one. Not really seeing his insecurities mirrored in the men outside. Men who had much more fearsome things to face than he did.

Instead he changed the subject. "So, explain how you could live at university without being exposed…um, you know what I mean."

"I didn't live on campus but in an apartment house with other students. Most of them older who had more of their classes complete. The place always smelled of boiled cabbage and formic acid. I don't know if it was a carry-over of working with treated animal cadavers or if they were trying to make blue ruin. Either way, I swear I could smell it on me for months after I received my credentials and left that place."

"Hum-m-m, could have been both, I suppose. So, you never spent time in the living quarters at university?"

"No, they didn't seem to have that whole caste system of having the younger classmen working like drudges for the uppers. Or if they did, it wasn't prevalent. I know some of the students needed to earn money for food and such in the apartments. There weren't any cooking facilities or anything like that. Aunt Laura kept me in enough funds so I ate in the public houses."

"But no valet, of course, so how did all that get done?"

She looked over at him strangely. "I suppose that brings out a difference in class between us. None of the students had valets that I know of. There were places that did our laundry and pressing and such. I had my hair cut short when I first left for Scotland."

"Your hair…?" He couldn't believe she had cut her hair but, of course, how could she have kept that glorious mass hidden.

"It's only hair, my lord. It grew back as you see. It was actually very freeing and there are times I wish I had it shorn again. When I first returned to London, I wore a wig to cover the fact my hair was so short but then I began to worry it had become infested with fleas from one of my patients."

He laughed. He couldn't help it. She was such a hoyden at times. Perhaps she said such things only to see what reaction he would give. He watched her through narrowed eyes to see if she knew what she did to him with her words.

When he refused to give her any response she could jump on, she continued. "I found wearing turbans, which my aunt owned several of, solved the dilemma. And the goats and sheep didn't seem half as interested in them as they had my wig or bonnets."

They both sat sipping their drinks, quietly enjoying the companionship even with no words being said. Finally, he asked, "Are you happy with your life?"

He thought she wasn't going to answer him. Possibly thought it too personal, too nosey.

"I enjoy who I am without all the rigmarole of titles or labels. I don't mind if others think of me as a spinster or blue-stocking or even shocking. I am my own person. I made myself what I am with the help of a very doting aunt but I wouldn't have it any other way. I am glad that I can help other living things. I am humbled I am allowed to help those men out there." Her head nodded to the east end of the house. "And I realize I am blessed with knowing those around me and how much they helped me become the woman I am."

"Well said, Miss Woods. I wish I were as sure about who I am as you are."

"It took me a while before I knew myself. As I said, Aunt Laura helped me understand my strengths and my abilities and that I didn't need to squish myself into some premade mold to be happy. In fact, she told me happiness would never be found if I tried to do so." Finishing her drink, she stood and left one finale sally. "I think she has always regretted that she didn't do more than she did to flaunt society. I helped her live out her fantasy, allowed her to see what a female can do when given the chance."

He stayed on. He certainly didn't wish to be seen escorting her upstairs at this time of night. At any time, come to think of it. He wasn't sure if she didn't say some of the things she did merely to get a rise out of him. To thwart what she knew were his convictions, his beliefs about women and their place in society. A woman was a woman and a man was a man.

Did he question that young men should be allowed to go off to university while young woman remain in the confines of their families? No, never. Young ladies needed the guidance and protection of their male relatives. Look what Cassie had got up to on her own. Or with only her aunt as a guide.

He had to admit he found her interesting and at times almost mesmerizing but Cassie was difficult to relax around. Made him unsure what she would say next. Made him edgy in his own skin. No, he decided he didn't care for how she made him feel at all.

Now if he could stop thinking about her, he would be able to believe it.

Finally catching his houseguest, Quinn raised his voice to gain her attention. "Miss Woods, may I presume on your time and have you inspect a flock of sheep one of my tenants is worried about? My gamekeeper has looked at them, but he isn't sure if they're ill," Quinn explained.

"Certainly, my lord. I'll get my bag and be right out." She headed to the front of the house.

Quinn acknowledged the men who were paying court to Cassie and noted his dog, his own dog, hardly raised his head at Quinn's voice. However, seemed ready to jump off the bed and follow Cassie until she put out one open palmed hand and said quietly, "Stay."

No puppy whines or squirms just complete abeyance. He wondered if she would use the same technique on him as he followed after her.

Cassie was beside the buggy Quinn ordered brought around and he helped her into it. She was such a controversy he couldn't help but smile. Wearing a simple grey dress similar to the one he first saw her in now covered by a crisp white apron, half-boots, which he saw when she got into the buggy and a completely bare straw hat with short ribbons to hold it on, she was the epitome of a dairy maid . Yet she appeared beautiful and Quinn felt lucky to have her sit beside him.

Cassie must have noted Quinn's glance at her bonnet, which had seen better days. "I took off the flowers and ribbons, well they were taken off for me by a goat. All those little nibbling animals can't seem to tell the difference between real and cloth flowers or they don't care. Either way, I didn't think the dye and such was good for them so I always wear an unadorned chapeau while attending to my patients now. The same with these gloves. If I don't hide them there will be holes chewed through them before we leave." He noticed she smiled at the thought. There was no rancor that her 'patients' dictated her ensemble.

As Quinn drove the buggy to the tenant's farm, alone with Cassie since he had dispensed with etiquette and left the tiger at the manor, he relaxed and told her about the various tenants and their cattle and what each field would be used for.

Cassie, as usual was full of questions and spoke knowingly of this type of farming and soil. They were soon at the farm and she hopped down from the buggy turning to retrieve her bag.

The farmer and his wife came out of the shed and welcomed them, apologizing for their appearance in their daily work clothes. Cassie brushed their concerns away and Quinn realized her appearance was a well-planned part of who and what Cassie was. She socialized with people who worked for a living, whose animals were next to their children in their worry and care. He gained new respect for her knowledge of people as well as her knowledge of animals. Turning, he followed the group into the stone-sided out-building.

The shed's inside was exactly as it looked outside. Fresh straw was on the ground and animal droppings were already festooned across the floor. Having removed her gloves and pushed them into a pocket under the apron, Cassie got down on one knee and took several of the sheep in turn. Studying their eyes, gently pulling open their mouths to see their lips and tongue, then checking their ears, she spoke to each one talking silly things like how were they feeling as if they would answer and make her job easier.

Standing up, she smiled at the worried farmers. "I don't think they have anything contagious. They're not running a fever and their eyes are nice and clear. I got a strong whiff of garlic so I would suggest you check the grasslands they were in for wild garlic. I would like to walk the fields they were last pastured in, also. I didn't like the look of some of their tongues." She followed the farmer out the side door and into a pasture.

Cassie walked slowly around the perimeter. She went down an embankment toward the stream that meandered through the property and bent and began pulling up some small plants. "Here's the culprit, I think. It begins as a plant appearing like Queen Anne's Lace but is actually giant hogweed. Quite poisonous and probably floated down the stream to take root here sometime this spring. This and poison yew berry plants are very appealing to grazing animals. Usually sheep are smart enough not to eat it, but this early in the spring, before the grasses have returned, they sometimes eat anything sprouting."

The relieved tenants thanked Cassie and Quinn, although they were a little reserved with their thanks to Quinn, not knowing how to address him or whether to offer their dirty hands to shake. Quinn noticed they were not hesitant with Cassie and warmly invited her back for lamb pie one day, which she graciously agreed to doing.

Cassie washed her hands at the water-trough and shook them dry before climbing into the buggy. Quinn had taken her medical bag from her and placed it on the floorboards already. The farmers waved a last goodbye and Quinn flicked the reins calling out, "Walk on."

He turned to watch her smile fade. "You enjoyed that, didn't you? Even getting down into the muck?"

"Well, that is where my patients are. I am glad it was simply a case of bad dining decisions and not a parasite or wasting disease. The loss of a flock that large would be devastating for a farmer. It would take them years to recover, if then. I am relieved not to have to give them that sort of bad news."

Quinn rode in silence thinking about having to live hand-to-mouth, having to depend on the vagaries of the weather and animals and countless other hardships he knew tenant farmers went through. He turned to Cassie to ask about the farmers' prosperity around Littleton and saw silent tears running down her cheeks.

He immediately pulled the horse to a stop. "My dear, Miss Woods. Why are you so distressed? The sheep are all right, aren't they?" At her nod, he asked again, "Then please tell me what the matter is. Is there some way I can relieve your mind of any worry or fear?"

"No, I'm being foolish wasting tears on things I had

no hand in and cannot change." She fumbled under her apron and pulled out a clean hankie. "I usually do not cry but when I do, Christopher says it is not pretty, so I apologize to you in advance, my lord." And with that bent her head to her knees and wept soundly.

Quinn was nonplussed. Sitting there in an open buggy on a public road with a weeping, no make that sobbing, young woman. He glanced about and thought, *'what the hell, in for a penny...'* He took Cassie by the arm and gently pulled her closer to him so she could lean against his shoulder and have her cry. A wet shoulder was the least of what he would contend with not to feel so helpless. Soon she was pulling away and sitting straighter in the seat, little hiccups replacing the racking sobs of earlier.

"I am so sorry, Lord Hedley. I should not have forgotten myself in such a way." She apologized while wiping her eyes again.

"Call me, Quinn, since I feel that your wetting my coat through to my shirt constitutes more than merely a polite relationship with one another." Then continued, "I may have to face another barrage of tears, but that wasn't about a flock of sheep. So, tell me, what has made you so melancholy?"

"I wished everything could be that easy, like the sheep. Keep them out of the field and all would be well again. But some things will never be well again. All those men at the manor and all those others throughout England will never be well again. They saw more death than anyone should. They faced death more times than anyone should. Yet, I expect them to pick-up the pieces they have left and march on to another battle." She flopped her hands in the air in frustration or mute plea.

"And it is a battle, I realize that, but I keep hoping they never do. Not until they are at least strong enough to feel the fight is worth the reward."

She gazed into Quinn's eyes and asked, "Do you understand what I'm saying. I know it's probably a hash, but I thought if anyone would understand it would be you." She hung her head in sorrow.

He felt she had reached into his soul and found his worry. "I know how helpless I feel when I look out over the pavilion and see all those young men, many younger than myself, and realize it is only a small percentage of the wounded. Men who will need jobs, men who need to return to normal lives with wives and children, and I feel overwhelmed. I finally took advice from Colonel Lancaster. I started taking one day at a time and one man at a time. I try to help at least one returning soldier a day. I have hired extra at each of my holdings."

He wanted her to feel better, wanted to see her smile. "My butler in London says if he has to train and find a situation for one more of my 'strays' he is going to find another placement for himself. Then another ex-soldier comes to the back door and he brings him in, feeds him, clothes him and trains him into service. I don't think he can stop himself at this point any more than I can."

He took hold of both her shoulders and faced her to him. "But Cassie, I know I didn't cause this war, I didn't send these men into battle, and I didn't wound them. All I can take blame for, is if I did not help them now. No one can ask more of themselves than that. No one is expecting more than that."

Cassandra gazed into Quinn's face and leaned toward him. Quinn answered by bending his head as he covered her mouth with his. His arms went around her shoulders, pulling her closer to his chest. He pulled away taking a deep breath then returned to her lips to drink from her sweetness, to get succor from her as well as to give it.

She returned the kiss as she learned the subtle movements involved and when his tongue entered between her lips, Cassie's own tongue met it with renewed energy. Quinn began rubbing her back, feeling the thin fabric covering even thinner fabric underneath. He started to pull away, giving her time to recover her composure, leaving him to wonder if he would ever recover his.

He gave three little kisses to Cassie's lips. "There, that should kiss it better." Searching her face to derive her feelings that seemed conflicted, Quinn turned facing forward and gave the horse the signal to continue home.

Quinn spent the time trying to get his breathing back to normal and to get his body under control. What started as empathy and condolence turned quickly to desire. Quinn wasn't sure how that happened. But one thing he did know, Christopher was wrong. Cassie was beautiful when she cried.

Cassie felt weighed down by concern. All the soldier's stories were the same yet different. All were afraid to cause pain to their family and loved ones when they had to tell them they were blind, some having amputations as well. All of them felt the loss of comrades who hadn't made it back home at all and had been left in some field in Spain. All of them had so much guilt—feeling they should have done things differently or better or sooner so that others would have lived.

The guilt, Cassie felt, was the hardest, went the deepest, and was the most difficult for the men to overcome. She often pointed out that their companions would feel the same if things were reversed and they were the ones sitting in the cots under the tents. It was all right to feel good about being alive and being able to return to their families and homes. No matter how thankful they were to be alive, there would be days when they would howl at the moon and rant against fate for what happened to them – to all of them.

One recent arrival, early on in Cassie's time at the Hall, was so despondent that all were worried he might take his own life if he found a way. Cassie, as usual, confronted the man and began to talk. "I understand you are a married man, sir."

"I mean you no disrespect, Madam, but I am asking you to leave me alone." The man did not turn toward her voice.

Not expecting a warm welcome, Cassie pulled a chair over to his bedside and made a great deal of sitting and getting her skirts just so, while the man on the cot let out a long, exasperated sigh.

Cassie smiled to herself then continued, "I understand that you will recover from your wounds to your leg and arm, that both were lacerations from a saber. I understand that meant you were injured during hand to hand combat." Without receiving any sort of answer, she kept on. "An officer then. I understand an officer is not often in the midst of battle, unless his men are being overcome."

The man finally reached out to where he knew she was, grabbing her wrist tightly and practically growled, "Woman, you may think you understand a lot of things, but you don't know a damn thing about what I or my men went through that day!"

She came right back at him heatedly. "Then why don't you tell me about it? I'm here and I'm ignorant and I want to know."

He threw her arm away as if it burnt him, snarling, "No you don't. I don't even know what happened that day. We were supposed to go in and stand our ground. When the enemy came at us, a troop of our soldiers would appear from our left flank and we would have the enemy pinned between us."

Cassie bit her lip and encouraged him to speak more about his last battle. "But that isn't what happened? The relief troop didn't show on time?"

"They Goddamned didn't show at all! I told my men…explained to them that we would fight like demons trying to get out of hell and draw the enemy to us. And then they would be rescued. We would have twice enough men to do the job…." The last few words died off into silence.

"I am sorry you and your men were put into such a perilous and compromising position, but it sounds as if they fought like the blazes for you. They must have respected you quite a bit to go into a battle like that, act as bait."

He shook his head to negate her words, but it was for more than hearing her words spoken aloud. "They shouldn't have. I misled them. I put them into danger and eighty per cent of my men didn't come out alive. I'm a hell of a commander, that's what my epitaph should be. I led my men to their death."

"I don't see it that way. You said it yourself, you led your men. It wasn't as if you were hiding high and dry up on an overlooking bluff. You were right there with them, swinging your sword, cutting down as many of the enemy as you could to protect your men, your troops. You are angry at yourself while letting those who made the plans and failed to carry them out get away Scott free. I am not an officer, but I would want to know what the hell happened to those who were to back me up. Where were the troops I was promised?" She ended indignantly.

"It doesn't matter, I lost my troops, men who had been with me from the beginning. We had never faced anything so bloody, so fierce and yet they did me proud. Before I fell, we were holding our own praying for the fresh troops coming from our flank. But I failed them," he said with so much despair Cassie was afraid she had done more damage to the man then good.

"So, do you know what happened after you were injured? Where are the twenty percent who were left? Are they dispersed to other commanders now? Do you think they blame you for the loss? Do you wish to know their whereabouts? And what of the men who fell beside you? Do you want their families to know how bravely and against what odds they stood their ground? If you wash your hands of your command, who will do these things?"

"Who the hell are you, Ma'am? I'm not sure you're really here or if it is my mind bringing up a demon to provoke me beyond anything I have had to face and that list is long. At first, I thought you were a do-gooder, come to see the poor wretched wounded, but now I think you came in particular to goad me into doing what I should have thought to do the first time I became conscious." There was the sound of wonderment in his voice.

"I am here because I need to help in some way. You needed to be reminded you are still an officer and a gentleman and you have duties left undone. You can never recover if you cannot face what occurred, to you and your troops."

"I will admit I have left some things undone for too long. I will get someone to write to the families of my fallen men first. Then to the ones who were left alive, if their new commander hasn't killed them by now." He swung his feet off the side of the cot. "I'll get to the bottom of why my men were left high and dry to fend for themselves after having been assured of a second wave of troops."

Cassie smugly pulled the portable writing case closer to her side, saying, "That is exactly why I'm here, sir."

Quinn stood in the rose garden, the same rose garden where he watched Cassie have tea with the men. Cassie's troops. He heard them called that and they seem to be proud of the title. A proud regiment of tough men all a little in love with their commander. Hell, he sometimes thought he was in love with her. Moore was a lucky man, blind or not. But she was wasted on Moore. He was a nice enough gentleman, but still a boy in many ways. Quinn thought she needed more than 'nice'. She needed a strong man who would rein her in, someone to remind her of what was proper and what a lady should do and think.

Who was he trying to fool? If he had the good fortune of having Cassie for himself, he would wake up every morning thanking his lucky star and letting her do anything she pleased. Quinn wasn't sure who he felt sorrier for. For Moore because she was going to lead him on a merry chase or for himself because she wasn't.

# CHAPTER SIX

Cassie helped with a little of the daily grooming, trimming beards and mustaches, but shied away from actually trying to shave any of them, including Christopher who had always been clean shaven. Several valets were hired to attend to the men since Cassie brought up the issue to Lord Hedley. The men's uniforms were appearing much better, also.

"Well, I feel unworthy to be amongst such handsome and debonair gentlemen. Major, you are most splendid in your uniform this morning. Are you planning on going somewhere?" Cassie flirted easily with the officer who had lost both a kneecap and his sight to the war.

In some of their late-night walks in the garden, he divulged there had been a woman he had planned on asking for, but with his injuries had given up on ever marrying. Cassie was trying to show him any woman who loved a man would rather have the man home and with her in any shape than to live without him. It was an ongoing battle of wills. But Cassie knew what she would want if their places were changed, and she was making plans to force the Major to see what life could be if he would only believe in love.

"I rode across the river and then on into town. I seem to have my seat back so to speak. It felt…invigorating," he told her.

"That sounds splendid. Perhaps we should make a party of it sometime. What say you?" she asked the group of men surrounding her. There were some assents as to wanting to ride, to feel the freedom of going further than their own two feet could take them even if they couldn't see those places.

Sometimes, when one was blind it was so easy to forget that others were near, and this was Cassie's way of reminding them they were not alone. To remind the Major of the others in case he was going to get personal as they often did alone in the rose garden. She knew it would cause him embarrassment if the others learned of his fears and worries.

Cassie knew the Major had a yearning so strong to ride again it was an intense pain. His horse made it through the many battles without an injury and Cassie and the Major spoke about the miracle of that, long into the night. This was a momentous occasion and Cassie took pride in the Major's accomplishment as well.

"I am afraid I do not have a riding habit or I might be tempted to ride out with you some morning. Perhaps I should send for it. Then there would be no excuse since I have seen side saddles in the stable when we visit."

The major made a bow and said chivalrously, "I await your accompaniment, Miss Woods."

Their night walks were what kept him sane he had told her, having difficulty sleeping at night because it is what everyone else, all normal people, did. Instead, he found Cassie available to take long strolls with him, sometimes visiting Triumph, sometimes walking the driveway to the gate and back.

The Major knew Cassie didn't begrudge him this confidence or feel they were taking anything away from the other men by having this one on one time together. They spoke of many different subjects but nothing personal about his past life, or about before joining the service other than to say his parents were against it and his sister told him to do as he wished.

She wanted men to forget about what they could no longer do and, instead, think about all that they could. If sharing a few night-time hours with this man would help him recover and join the life he was meant to lead, then she would sacrifice a few hours of sleep. After all, this Major had lost so much by going into service for his country she couldn't see anyone misunderstanding. She felt if she could get this fiercely independent male to admit he needed something more, a woman by his side, she would think her time well-spent. Of all the men here, no one should be left to live in the past. In the what might have been.

She saw they were healing from their injuries. They were healing from fighting. They were healing from losing their sight. Now they needed to heal from the war within themselves. Learn to live as they once had or as closely to it as possible. She could not shirk her duty to see them all made whole and sent home. She wouldn't feel her work complete until the tents were empty and the constant flow of wounded ended.

Cassie added to her troop. New combat patients brought from the coastal towns to be seen by Dr. Landon were increasing as the fighting increased. It was rumored that the end of the war was near and that soon all the soldiers would be brought home.

The new, younger patients tended to treat Cassie much as they would a woman of their mother's age and she never disabused them of their thinking. It was better if they held the image of her as matronly. Then they wouldn't feel embarrassed by her being a younger woman or intimidated by being a lady in her own right.

The older, more seasoned men treated her as a lady and always were pleasant even if she knew they were in pain. It wasn't always easy for her to look at these broken men. However, knowing how well some of the first men she tended were doing made her own discomfort seem so insignificant as to disappear altogether.

She began with each new man as she had with Christopher. Learning who they were, what they did before the war, and what they wanted to do in the future. Dr. Landon must have agreed with her methods because he left her to her own devices and often made sure the orderlies and batmen knew she was to be obeyed.

Just as Cassie thought she was making great progress, or rather the men were, something pulled her back to her first few days at Hedley Hall. New members to the group starting from the beginning eventually blended with those already well into their recovery and acceptance of their blindness.

Many of the newer patients were still unsure if they would regain their sight and the doctor could not always diagnose permanent loss until some of the other injuries were healed. Blindness that affected the man's mind rather than his eyes were ones as that, which only time would tell.

Not an easy prognosis for some of these men, especially officers who were used to being in control, not hand-fed or bathed by someone else. It grated on their dignity and their sense of manliness.

Cassie had to tiptoe around these men until she learned more of their temperament and their anger at their predicament. She usually approached to invite them to listen with the group to her reading the newspaper or to inquire about writing letters home.

One such man had been there several days, an officer. In fact, one of their highest ranking. A Colonel and mean and cantankerous and rude. Cassie accommodated his attitude as she knew he was also frustrated.

In pain with every movement and mad as hell that after all his time in service he was wounded in the rear. His rear, his buttock, his bum. There was no other way to say it. He was forced to remain face down while blind in a bed in the middle of a tent full of men who were of lesser rank knowing all that went on with him.

All the rooms inside the wing of the house were occupied by men in more need. Other than the Major, along with his valet, who wasn't going to be placed into a tent at this late date.

Cassie was obligated to face the music again and approached the bad-tempered man with her writing box and asked politely as she always did, "Colonel? Is there a letter I could write for you today? Someone you would like to know where you are or how you are doing."

"No, but you can hold my pot for me so I can take a piss," he told her crudely.

"I'll call one of the orderlies for you…." she began.

When he added, "Well then you can hold my cock for me while I go. I'm sure you can handle that job, at least."

Cassie knew she should be shocked, but was beyond that after seeing and hearing what these men had been through. Instead, she tried to keep from laughing but didn't succeed. "If you think that's an offer, I cannot refuse, then you have not seen yourself from this angle, sir. I am afraid you must manage your own Johnson, because I assure you, I do not have the time it would take to find it. I'm more used to aiding Great Danes than English Spaniels."

There was complete silence all around. Cassie hadn't meant for anyone but the Colonel to hear her remark and was blushing now as she realized this exchange would be the talk of every one of the men for days.

Finally, the silence was broken by the Colonel's before unheard guffaws. He laughed so hard Cassie was afraid he wasn't going to be in need of that pot after all.

"Oh, I deserved that, I did. I'm just so ill-tempered I could spit. But really, ma'am. An English Spaniel? Give a man a little bit of something to cling to in this less than enviable position."

"Well, I usually castrate my male patients so if I were you, I'd settle for what I could get. I'm a licensed veterinarian and am helping here until the men stop flowing through Hedley Hall like the Thames." She informed him to lessen the sting of her remarks and to let him know she wasn't offended, but also wasn't a whipping boy.

"I knew some of the doctors in the field were more veterinarians than true medical men, but to have that brought home to me here is truly bad news," he told her half-joking.

"Just remember to behave yourself since I do have my bag and surgical implements with me." She waited while that news sank in and asked, "Now is there a letter you would like to dictate so the people back home will know you are feeling sprightlier?"

As she turned to pick up the portable letter-writing box, she saw Lord Hedley trying to hide a grin as one of the other men whispered to him. Cassie knew it was about what had just occurred and she wasn't sure she wanted to know the lord's opinion after his warning to her about keeping everything impersonal with the men.

She was relieved when he raised his head after hearing the story and one eyebrow shot up as he made a snipping motion with two fingers as if cutting with a pair of scissors. Cassie turned away before she laughed out-right at him or gave him the same warning as she gave the Colonel for being cheeky with her.

A few weeks later, the Colonel walked up to her and taking her hand said, "I have a lot to thank you for. Before you spoke a few home truths, I was wallowing in self-pity and thinking only about what I lost. You spoke to me like I was a child throwing a tantrum, saying anything that came into my head while everyone around me quaked in my displeasure. I can assure you I will never see a Great Dane without thinking of you." He smiled in self-depreciation.

"And I will think of you every time I see an English Spaniel," she returned raising one eyebrow in imitation of Lord Hedley.

"I am returning to my wife who has put up with my moods and I will give her a good buss on the cheek for doing so for all these years. I was unbearable although no matter how I tried I couldn't get away from myself. Now my, umm, wound is healed and my sight has returned. Dr. Landon felt it had to do with the blow to my head when a shell knocked me from my horse. I thank God, you, and the good doctor for seeing me well. You all did a part in making me a whole man again and in making me see myself through other's eyes. If you ever find I can do you a service, please do not hesitate to contact me. I will never retire from the cavalry. They will have to carry me off the field and I do not plan on letting that happen a second time."

"I'm so glad your sight has returned and you can resume your profession. I think in the long run you are a good commander and one who will always think of his troops now as more than pawns. Facing death and uncertainty can make everyman rethink his life's choices."

Lady Melanie stopped Cassie as she was leaving the breakfast room. This was the first-time Cassie had ever seen the lady without her husband at her side. Cassie turned and offered to return to the room, but Lady Melanie led her into an unoccupied parlor.

"I wanted to thank you for staying. I have heard wonderful things about what you are accomplishing with the patients. If Nathan had had someone like you, I think he would never have gotten so melancholy," Melanie told her.

"I understand he had trouble coming to grips with his loss of sight. Regaining some vision must have been a great help in his total recovery."

"You would think so but I think he felt guilty, too. He lashed out at everyone, even his brother who was only trying to help."

Cassie's expression of sympathy must have shown on her face.

Lady Melanie continued, "Oh, he wasn't physical, at least not to me. I am not sure Quinn and Nathan did not come to blows at some point. I do not know what happened, but suddenly, Nathan wanted to learn to live with his handicap. I bless that day, since it was before his sight began to improve. I give the credit to Quinn. It has been a long struggle and yet a short time. I have a more loving, appreciative husband than I married and I thank God every day."

Cassie sat thinking about what Lady Melanie told her. She knew this must refer to the time Nathan had gone to the woods and Lord Hedley had challenged him. "I am glad Nathan is now the man you want him to be. I am hoping I can help these other men get to the same place."

"If there is anything I can do, I would be more than happy to help."

"Well, Lady Melanie, if that is the case, I have been talking with the men...."

And with that, Lord Hedley would have been able to warn Melanie of the danger of Cassie's beginning any sentence with those words. But it would have been too late. Lady Melanie was caught in a net no one sees coming and one Cassie doesn't mean to throw.

# CHAPTER SEVEN

Cassie continued to find ways for the men to reenter society, reenter the lives they left when the war began. She set-up a plan where the plates were like the face of a clock. Meat would be placed at twelve o'clock followed by sides at three, six and nine. With a little help in cutting up meat and large vegetables, most of the soldiers could find and eat their meals on their own.

Taking tea became an art. Cassie would play mother and pour, adding the requested number of sugars or cream. When the recipient held their hand out, Cassie placed the saucer unto their palms. Then the saucer and cup could be raised to their mouth and there were no embarrassing spills. That is once the trick was learned. Cassie explained it was the honesty and openness of the blind to let the sighted know how to proceed.

"Once a sighted person, especially a hostess, is told what needs to be done so her guest can be comfortable, she is obligated to fulfill that need. Those of you with wives, they will learn this same method of service. It is no different than pouring tea or coffee for a sighted guest. Your part will be to gauge where your hostess is and be within arm's length so she can place the saucer, just so." She handed the saucer to the sergeant, placing it in his hand.

Cassie continued, "This is true whether you have use of both or just one arm. Simply accept the cup only. Your hostess will understand. Those with both hands, can expand into adding a biscuit or scone as you become more used to eating standing up holding a saucer and teacup. I am glad that, being a lady, I get to sit most of the time."

Cassie spoke to the whole group of men surrounding her. "I am having a small dinner party this evening for those of you who wish to attend. Nothing too formal, but we will set for at least five courses and removes. It will be good practice for dining with a commanding officer or your future wife's family. It will, of course, encompass some techniques we haven't covered yet. Eating at a table brings in more cutlery and glasses then we have been working with. Lord Hedley's butler has brought in a dining table and we will be served by the footmen and valets from our own staff so there will be no new people. Please come and enjoy the company. I understand there may be both wine and spirits offered."

A few hours later, her formal dinner was being served. Cassie, wearing her best dinner gown even though most of her guests couldn't see it, gazed down her table. She admired the handsome men who now felt comfortable enough to dress for dinner and eat in a manner most of them had done prior to their injuries. It seemed mostly officers were being sent to Hedley Hall to heal lately.

"Welcome, Gentlemen. I'm so glad you could attend this evening's festivities. I would suggest you make yourself comfortable with the place setting in front of you. There is a charger plate, which is removed at the first course. On the right, will be the knives and on the left the forks. Above twelve of the clock is the dessert spoon and to the right of that a water glass and a wine glass. The wine glass will be changed out with the various courses, but not its placement. If you have any questions, please feel free to ask. This is a learning exercise as well as a good meal to enjoy together."

As Cassie spoke, she saw most of the men were lightly touching and feeling their place settings. She continued, "The serviettes will be placed in your lap by the footmen and the meal will begin shortly. This is where you make small talk with the person next to you," she teased.

The first course was brought in and Cassie announced, "The first course is a chicken broth. No pesky vegetables to get in the way. You should listen for your hostess to begin. I think you can all hear me, but if not, you will hear when others have started eating so you then may begin to feel free to do so."

The meal continued in the same vein. She could see Lord Hedley watching from the doorway to the makeshift dining room. There were a few slips of missed food bites but the table cloth lived through the meal and not a drop of wine was spilled.

The lesson continued. "Usually a footman will announce what he is serving but if you are ever confronted with something you may not wish to eat in a public setting, such as fish with all the little bones, merely decline it or leave it on the plate untouched. The same as if you did not care for the item. It will be removed without comment and replaced with something hopefully you will be able to eat. It would be better to leave the table hungry than to embarrass yourself or, worse, get a fish bone stuck in your throat." With that the gentlemen surrounding her murmured their agreement.

After the meal was complete, Cassie announced, "There will be music in the room next door. Lady Melanie has offered to play some renditions of her favorites on the pianoforte. Gentlemen, I leave you to your brandy and port and will await you in the music room. The footmen will show you the way."

It wasn't long before the men entered the room and found seats facing the musical instrument. Lady Melanie began what turned out to be a very professional sounding musicale. Lady Melanie had offered her help and Cassie was more than pleased with the results. The audience applauded and even requested an encore, which Lady Melanie furnished with blushing cheeks.

Colonel Lancaster was sitting at the rear of the room the entire performance and Cassie glanced over at him several times throughout the evening. Each time the pride and love for his wife showed plainly on his face. Cassie thought how wonderful that must be, to be loved so thoroughly. One of those times she caught Lord Hedley watching her. Love didn't shine out of his eyes at Cassie, but she felt he was contemplating something seriously.

Cassie, too excited about the success of the night to sleep, slipped out to the rose garden where she often walked to think over her day's work. Many of the men had been very relaxed in the presence of Lady Melanie, speaking with her after the performance to give her their personal appreciation. If one closed one's eyes it had sounded exactly like any other societal dinner party. It was something she would repeat with the gentlemen on a regular basis, she decided, to make them comfortable around sighted people again.

Cassie heard footsteps on the path coming toward her. "Good evening, Doctor. Were you able to join us for the musicale? Lady Melanie is an accomplished artist. We must have her play for us more often in the future."

"Yes, Lady Melanie is a very fine musician. Tonight, made me think of London. You did a fine job of getting the patients to forget about their limitations and enjoy what they have been blessed with." The doctor seemed solemn as if there were other things on his mind.

Dr. Landon stopped walking and placed his hand on Cassie's sleeve. She turned toward him, looking up to see his eyes, which were visible due to the full-moon.

"Miss Woods, I must tell you of the high regard I have for you. I have watched these men, once simple patients, become so much more with a little understanding. I find I am searching you out, always finding you helping someone. I think of you as I go to sleep. I am beginning to be obsessed with you, and although I know it to be wrong, I dream of us being together. Please, please, Miss Woods, I am beside myself with admiration so strong I would break any vow, any rule of polite society if only you would agree to...." And the fine doctor could go no further before he bent to passionately kiss her.

Cassie quickly turned her head to the side and the kiss that was meant to show how much he desired her, instead became a chaste kiss of an uncle.

Cassie stepped aside. "I am honored by your regard, but I think it is one of propinquity rather than passion. Please except this in the manner to which it is given. Go home to your wife for a few days. You are in need of her comfort and presence. Now when we meet again, we will not speak of this. Blame the beautiful music, the good wine and a full moon in a night sky of stars."

The doctor was quiet for a few moments. Cassie could tell he was mortified and already regretting what he had said and done. He bowed. "My pardon, Miss

103

Woods. I was over-set by the evening's events." Then turned swiftly and left the garden toward the manor house.

Cassie thought to herself, *I never saw that coming.* From one of the men, possibly. They could easily misconstrue gratitude for a deeper feeling, but a married man, a doctor, had Cassie rethinking her relationships with everyone at the manor. But she was certain the doctor was missing his wife and had placed those warmer feelings toward the only unmarried woman nearby. The man spent all day with the patients and so any softer female traits were as a beacon to him.

Cassie was still in contemplation when she felt another's presence. She looked up from the path and said, relieved, "Oh, hello, Major. It was a wonderful evening wasn't it. It felt quite like London during my come-out."

Expecting a similar reply from the Major, Cassie was again surprised that evening when instead he said, "Miss Woods, Cassie, I must tell you of my deep esteem."

She felt herself tensing, this cannot be happening again. So soon. But the Major continued even though she was wishing with all her might he stop talking and go away.

"I wish to make my declaration…." he began.

"Major," she interrupted. "Please leave me and sleep on this decision you are about to make." She began making her way to the front path hoping her words had put a stop to his.

"Miss Woods, I have thought about it, almost every day, all day. I know we suit each other very well. We are both quick thinking, enjoy conversation about the world, enjoy good literature and I find you very, very attractive. I want and need you. I love you," he confessed.

She again stopped and turned to the man and allowed him to take her hands in his. She squeezed them in response. "I think you have gone through the most traumatic time of your life and felt adrift for so long, I became as a lifeboat to a drowning man. I appreciate the honor you do me, but please remember your life. The one you must return to as the eldest son. The one where you told me there had been an understanding between you and the special woman in your life." Cassie reasoned with him hoping her words would remind him of his duties, his mandated future.

"I don't care about that past life. We can go anywhere and make a fine life together. I know you care for me. I can hear it in your voice," he said earnestly.

"I think of you as a very special man. One I find very attractive and one I love. But not in a carnal way. I cannot think of you as a husband. As a good friend, as a brother, yes, but not as a lover," she said softly.

"It is not because I am blind. I know you do not judge a man by his handicaps, but will you not think on it? Give me hope?" he asked, almost pleading.

"I don't need to think on it. I love you as a brother. I cannot think of you in a more romantic encounter. Please sleep on this and in the morning, you will know I am right," she told him quietly.

"May I kiss you? To prove to you there is more between us then friendship? Please," he whispered his plea.

"Yes, of course, why would I turn down a kiss from a close friend?" And with that she turned her face up to his as one of his hands closed lightly over her cheek, holding her head so he could find her lips.

*Well,* thought Cassie*, he certainly isn't kissing me like a sister or a friend.* She could tell there was experience and passion in the kiss and he wasn't holding back. His lips moldered to hers, softer than she would have thought yet seeking more from her. His tongue skimmed across her lips asking for entry which she accepted. The kiss was deepened and Cassie thought *I could get used to this.* It was somewhat pleasant, but not earth shattering.

The Major finally lifted his head and said, "That was nice, very, very nice."

"But was it as nice as the kiss you were comparing it to?"

"A gentleman does not kiss one lady while thinking about another. You wound me," he stepped back from her.

"Then tell me that during that kiss you did not think about your former betrothed?" Cassie demanded he be honest with her if not with himself.

"This is why I love you," he said, accepting the brush off with grace. "Who else would tell me I don't know my own mind and that I love someone else, no matter if the words break my heart."

"I did not break your heart. Now go to bed and I will talk with you in the morning. I am beginning to get a crick in my neck from staring up at you." She scolded him like the sister she felt herself.

The Major was out of her sight when another shadow paused in her path.

"Oh, Lord Hedley, you startled me. I was just going in," Cassie said as she went to go around him on the path.

"Why? Do you have another clandestine meeting

with yet another of your lovers?" he asked with a final hiss.

Although not understanding why, Cassie knew he was holding on to his temper tightly and was close to bursting with pent up anger. "I think it has been a long day for all of us. Do you mind if we talk more in the morning?" she said trying to reach his reasonable side.

"By morning there will be so many men in line for your favors, we would need to draw straws." He grabbed her by the shoulders and dipped his head towards her lips.

"My lord!" There, those two damning words she used like a lance. "You should remember we are not alone."

Although he glanced around, he saw no one close. "It's dark, no one can see us." And he began his descent towards her lips again.

"It is always dark for some of us. Please, remember who you are." She admonished sternly.

With that statement, Lord Hedley dropped his hands from her arms and with a bow, apologized, "Miss Woods, please forgive me. I forgot myself for a moment." And with that he slipped into the darkened shadows of the house and was gone.

She stood motionless, taking deep breaths for a moment then said quietly, "Gentlemen, let us keep the events of this evening to ourselves, shall we?" Then she too walked toward the manor house.

There were murmurs of agreement as she left.

# CHAPTER EIGHT

Cassie was angry, so very angry at Lord Hedley. How could the man be that dense! He was more blind then the men without sight. How dare he reprimand her actions. He wasn't her father, for God's sake. Why did it matter how many men she met out in the garden? What was it to him? Cassie took the time during her walk to the house to contemplate what had occurred between Lord Hedley and herself. By the time she got to the front door she had made a decision. It may be rather bold, but Cassie felt Aunt Laura would approve.

After finding out the direction of Lord Hedley, Cassie proceeded down a hallway to his private library. She had been there before so she opened the door to see Lord Hedley leaning with his arm on the top of the fireplace contemplating the dead ashes. He stood upright when he realized she entered the room and before he could say anything, Cassie turned the key in the lock, ensuring their privacy.

"You should not be in here alone with me."

"You mean to worry about my reputation after all the clandestine meetings I've had, my lord?" she asked with untypical nonchalance.

"Quinn," he said. "Call me Quinn, and I have already apologized. I should not have said anything untoward to you. I should not have put my hands on you." He seemed ashamed at his loss of control.

"I understand some of it, I think."

"How can you, when I don't understand it myself.

Are you trying to tell me you know me better than I know myself?" he asked crossly. "Why I should care what a piece of baggage like you does, how many hearts you break or how many lives you ruin, is beyond me. But I feel responsible for any damage you do to these men. I brought you here knowing what you were. I knew you were betrothed to Moore and then broke his spirit. Yet, I let you stay and worm your way into everyone's heart."

"I was never any of those things." Cassie stated quietly. If she were to make any progress with this discussion, she would need to make sure it did not escalate into an angry confrontation.

"You weren't what? Engaged? Untrue to your vows?" he asked sarcastically.

"I have never been engaged." Another statement.

"But you told me you were engaged to Lieutenant Moore," he accused glaring straight at her, daring her to lie.

"No, you told me I was engaged to Lieutenant Moore. I decided to come to him when you told me he was injured and was asking for me. I didn't need to know anything else to come to his aid."

"Then what is he to you? He welcomed you with open arms."

"He is a neighbor. His mother is my aunt's close friend and he's engaged to a village girl, named Lucy. She is caring for his mother. I hope to get him to return to his home as soon as he is ready."

He slammed his fist down on the mantle. "I saw you tonight. I saw you kissing man after man. I was outraged!"

"You saw man after man kissing me. There is a difference and the doctor's hardly counted since I have had more passionate kisses from grateful pets nursed back to health." She felt she answered reasonably. "The doctor is missing his wife. Proximity confused him. I suggest you invite Mrs. Landon for an extended visit until the doctor has more time to travel home."

Quinn watched Cassie, trying to read more into her words than she was saying. Was it all a mistake? Was she playing him like a fish, letting out the line then drawing it taught again? Was he a bigger fool than he already felt? Or was he willing to make excuses for her? Accept any reason simply to allay his fear of losing her? To keep her within his sphere and his sight. This young woman had confused and confounded him from the moment they met.

"I'm sorry, I may, umm, I have misunderstood occurrences of today. But you can't deny you flirt outrageously with every officer down to the lowest ranking foot soldier," he stated as if this fact redeemed him for thinking poorly of her.

Cassie looked at him as she would a dumb animal. "I flirt with those men to remind them they are still men. A man never feels more handsome, more masculine, and more alive than when he is flirting. I could resemble a sea-hag and they would respond to my teasing and banter. I enjoy making them feel good about themselves and I enjoy their flirting in return. It enhances my vanity even though I know they don't know what I look like. I'm getting them to think about loved ones at home. Getting them to want to heal and get back to their lives. It is innocent and has never gone beyond what is acceptable."

"What about tonight? What about the Major?" he asked, the anger returned to his voice.

"The Major. What can I say?" she said slowly. "I worry that I should have seen that coming somehow. He is hiding from his past, his life as he knows he must live it. He is an eldest son. He has an estate and a young woman waiting for him to come home to and marry. He is finally realizing where his life and heart lies, yet still fights against it. He is trying to find a way around returning to what he must. I think he will be leaving us soon."

"After kissing you like that? I should call him out!" he said emphatically.

Cassie chuckled. "With what? Pistols? That sounds a little unfair to me. Possibly after nightfall? Bow and arrows? He may have more of a chance with that, but I do not know where I would attach the windmill on your person," she said casually.

Quinn felt his mouth twitching, as he pictured the newspaper headlines. Talk about a less than desirable situation. Even shooting the arrow into the air wouldn't save face following that duel.

"All right, you win. I am overly sensitive. I'm not sure why I have been so edgy lately," he confessed rubbing the back of his neck.

"I'm not sure what is between us either, but it has been there since you first burst through the brush and looked at me with surprised pleasure in your eyes," Cassie said bluntly.

"You have felt it, too? I thought I was going a little bit mad. I put it down to stress and to being protective of Moore. He seemed so young for you to be interested in." Quinn finally admitted his doubt out loud.

111

"He is young. I was the older sister he didn't have. I enjoyed wading in the stream and catching tad poles, exploring Roman ruins, and playing with slimy stuff under a microscope. He was the perfect playmate for me every summer I spent with Aunt Laura. My father thought she would be the female role model I needed. Little did he realize what a modern thinker his sister had become. Ergo, I became a doctor of veterinary science instead of a quiet country wife." She walked closer, touching the back of a chair where she stopped, almost within reach. "Christopher and I did everything together until I went away to London for my come-out and then university while he went into service."

"Why didn't you simply explain this all to me when I came to bring you to Hedley Hall?"

"Would you have brought me if you had known the truth? That there wasn't more than friendship between Christopher and me? Once hearing Christopher had asked for me, I wasn't about to abandon him. I needed to find out why he had done so."

"And that was….?"

"He didn't wish his mother or Lucy to know about his blindness. He feared what so many of these men fear. That their families won't want them back. That they will be turned away or treated as a millstone. They feel what your brother felt so strongly."

"But then you stayed."

"I have decided to live a life different from what I was born into. I hate that women are limited to so few choices in life. That they go from being their father's daughter to being their husband's wife with no voice at all. Then they become someone's mother and it begins all over again." This wasn't the conversation she thought they would be having. How did things become so complicated? All she had wanted was to be kissed by a man she felt more than fondness for. "I wish you had told me. I feel like a fool," he said abashedly.

"You are a fool," she said teasingly. "Are you going to kiss me or am I going to have to do that, too?"

"You pushed me away. Now you want me to kiss you?" he asked laughingly.

"I pushed you away because you were kissing me in anger. A kiss should never be in anger. A kiss is a messenger of forgiveness, sympathy, friendship, love—but never anger," Cassie explained waiting for him to come closer to her.

Quinn pulled her toward him. Spreading his legs, he made room for her body to fit perfectly between them. Bending his neck to accommodate the difference in their height, he captured her waiting lips.

*Now this was a kiss!* That was all Cassie could think before succumbing to the warmth of his lips, the light sucking of her lips into his, the light nipping and coaxing for her to open her mouth and give him entrance into the warmth waiting there for him. Quinn's arms that were encircling her, holding her to him, to all the parts that were available to touch her were now stroking down her back and round to her bottom.

Cassie turned outward, coaxing Quinn to bring a hand around between them. She didn't know what she wanted, but she wanted more touching. She started to rub her entire body against his, up and down, up and down.

"God, Cassie, you're killing me! Are you a virgin?" He whispered the question while snuggling into the warm curve of her neck, lightly sucking the soft creamy skin there.

The question was like a splash of cold water in her face. Remembered conversations with Aunt Laura flooded back into her memory. Conversations about the inequalities of the system. Men, even after marriage can do anything, but a woman must remain faithful to her vows. Society painted the woman in any bad marriage as the one who was in the wrong—she didn't try hard enough, she didn't perform her duties well enough, or she wasn't passionate enough. A sick feeling deep in her stomach made Cassie push herself away to stand on her own.

The coolness between them finally sank into Quinn and he asked, "What's wrong?"

Cassie asked confrontationally, "What if I said I wasn't a virgin?"

Quinn tried to pull her back into position and began to nuzzle her neck and place little sucking kisses against her skin again, but mumbled through the kisses, "I'd like to kill the son of a bitch for hurting you because I know you wouldn't have made love without being fully enamored. But at the same time, I'd like to shake his hand for leaving you so I could have you." All the time kissing and sucking between the words.

Cassie sank in to lean between Quinn's legs again. She was innocent of ever being with a man, but the years of medical school left no misunderstanding as to what making love included. She could feel Quinn's erection quite plainly. The size was a little daunting, but she knew the human body was made to accommodate the act.

She felt she should be honest with Quinn before things got away from her. She was really liking everything he was doing and she was having a difficult time coming up with any reason not to make love with him right here on his library rug.

"I am," she said as Quinn tried to take over her lips again. Kissing and sucking and drawing his tongue over the seam between the two. Wanting in.

He asked, "Am what?" And returned to concentrating on her lips.

"I am a virgin," she told him bluntly.

Quinn pulled away and stared her straight in the eyes.

She explained, "I thought you should know. I didn't want it to come as a surprise."

Quinn smiled and said quietly, "I appreciate the warning." Then he went back to kissing her and stroking her body into submission.

A loud rapping on the library door as someone tried to turn the doorknob interrupted their dalliance. A panicked young boy was calling, "Miss Cassie, Miss Cassie!"

Quinn lifted his head and smiled ruefully. "I think you are being summoned." He stood and set her away from him reluctantly. "I don't know if I am grateful or resentful." Their gazes met. "Ask me later."

Cassie tried to pat her hair into some acceptable manner while hurrying to unlock the door to see what was wrong.

Barely getting the door open, Jessie, the stable boy said excitedly, "Oh, Miss Cassie. The Major's horse is hurt. We can't get the bleeding stopped and they say something about a tendon being cut and we may have to put the horse down. Oh, miss, please come and help. The Major loves that horse."

"Let me grab my bag and I'll be right there," she said as she turned with pleading eyes for Quinn to understand.

"Go, go. I'll bring your bag. Do you need anything else?"

"No, I'll get water from the stable pump."

Cassie arrived at the stall to see several men in various state of dress, evidently many of them having retired for the evening, bending over the hind leg of the Major's horse. The Major himself was entering from the other end of the stable with Jessie leading his way. Cassie noted the worry that was causing the Major's brows to furl, but she couldn't offer any words of encouragement until she had time to access the injury herself.

"Here there, make room for Miss Cassie, you lugs. She needs to see what's what," ordered the stablemaster. Cassie had helped at the stable when asked. One time helping a horse with bloat and another time with a breach foal. Both incidents ending well. The grooms were very appreciative of her help and accepted her into their private domain readily.

Kneeling, she removed the bloody rag wrapped around the hind leg of the agitated animal. There was a gash on the inside of the leg that pulsed blood every time the heart beat.

"Try to sooth him if you can, Major," she instructed. "I'll have to ask all the rest of you to stand back out of sight so Triumph will calm down. He is in pain and he isn't sure which one of you to blame."

The head-groom must have thought that meant someone was to blame and started to explain how he searched for any loose nails sticking out or pieces of wire not cut back. Cassie was tearing off more strips from a new piece of cloth explaining, "I wasn't placing blame.

I know you care for these horses as if they were your babes. But the horse can't think like that. He only knows he is in pain and we are all here to take our share of the responsibility. He is really not going to like me when I get finished."

Quinn showed up and handed the bag to Cassie who opened it. She knew suturing the gash wouldn't stop the bleeding if an artery was nicked. The horse had lost a lot of blood and Cassie worried about doing surgery on a weakened horse while it was conscious. Using chloroform was a dangerous proposition on this large of an animal and might cause Triumph to die during the procedure.

Cassie peered under the cloth she had applied and tied to cover the gash and found, gratefully, the bleeding had slowed. Suturing should be all that was needed. Then making sure the horse didn't get a fever or the wound to fester would be their most urgent worry.

"Hold his head, Major. I'm going to suture this and Triumph will probably be more nervous of me being down here than the actual sutures. He isn't going to like, well, let us just say he isn't going to like anything much for the next half hour." Cassie began the dangerous job of mending Triumph.

It was well into the early morning when Cassie finally gave her last instructions. "Put one more row of hay piles along this side to make the stall too narrow for Triumph to move around much. And did you get all the mares out of here? We don't need one of them going into season and have Triumph tear out all the hard work we did."

The stable boy and grooms accepted her commands as if they came from the Major himself. No one questioned Cassie or her orders.

Quinn said quietly, "Let's get you to bed." Then murmured just for her ears, "Alone, but don't remind me I said that tomorrow. I'll deny saying any such thing."

They walked together up to the house, entering through the side door. Both said goodnight at the same time then grinned at each other. Cassie headed for her room upstairs and Quinn went towards the library. "I'll stay down here for a while. I don't feel I have the strength of character not to follow you to your room so I could show my appreciation of your skills."

Cassie went to her room and striped off the ruined gown. She sat staring at her reflection in the mirror. Working on Triumph put paid to her hairstyle. There was even straw sticking out of the once neat chignon. Picking up the brush she tried to bring some semblance to the rat's nest. She was glad she hadn't accepted the offer of a lady's maid because now she could take this time and think about the evening.

To say she had a lot to think about was an understatement. First, Dr. Landon surprised her with his announcement of love followed by the Major's declaration. Both, she thought, came unexpectedly. The doctor's attention she easily understood. He was lonely and missing his wife.

The major was a different story. In all the talks and walks and rides with the Major, he had never shown any signs of declaring himself. And he should not have in her opinion. They were miles apart in social station and, if he were honest with himself, their attraction to each other. Not that he was unattractive, but marriage needs a special passionate desire to make it strong enough to survive the tribulations of life.

She hadn't thought she would be facing these kinds of issues tonight. Instead, she hoped that when she was approached by Lord Hedley, she would find he realized his error of thinking her a flirt. She knew it was unfair of her to think he would somehow come upon this information on his own. She knew Christopher would never say anything in fear that if Cassie had no male here to care for, she would be sent home.

Chris wasn't ready to go home and face the life that waited for him there. The uncertainty of meeting Lucy as a blind man and then his widowed mother would be too much. He was her only child and was supposed to take-over the running of the farm once he sold out of the infantry and went home to marry.

Cassie thought about Quinn. She shivered remembering him whispering in that husky voice to call him, Quinn. It was a lovely name, a lovely voice, and lovely man. She held the brush to her breasts and remembered how she felt when he touched her there. How his mouth felt, how he tasted, how he seemed to want even more of her.

She wasn't sure what that meant, but she thought she wanted to find out. To return to his arms and allow him to finish what he had begun to teach her. In the reflection of the mirror, she saw the way her own eyes changed as she thought of being held in his arms, kissed and fondled. If she never received anything more from this man, she would remember this night.

She picked up the dress. Between kneeling in Triumph's stall and the blood from the injury, no amount of cleaning would save it. She wasn't sorry. She never went to places that required such a dress any longer.

Removing the rest of her clothes, she glanced at her

naked body in the mirror quickly before pulling on her nightgown. She knew her body but right now she needed to be more circumspect and not think about what could have happened if the stable boy hadn't come searching for her that evening. How her life, her very being, would have changed.

Where had all her principles gone? The plan for her life? The vow never to allow a man to take control of her? Aunt Laura would be so disappointed that the first attractive man Cassie came in contact with was able to over-come all her resistance. If there had been any resistance, that is, perhaps Cassie wouldn't be feeling such a traitor to the female species.

Instead, she had melted into his arms. Accepted his kisses and fondling like some obsessed paramour. Where were all her high-morals? Her dedication to her values and her worth as a person and not merely an extension of a man?

She wasn't her father's daughter, Lady Casandra. She vowed never to be some man's wife and exchange her name for his. Her self-respect for his title. She had made a promise to herself never to be some man's chattel and she almost threw away all her principles for one night of bliss.

# CHAPTER NINE

Cassie was sitting in the largest tent with her troop. The new additions to the patient rolls were being housed in the newly emptied rooms in the east wing where the dinner was normally held. The number of newly injured seemed to have slowed so that meant either the battles were not as vicious or there were not as many survivors. Cassie hoped it was the former.

She made her usual number of announcements before the morning reading session. "This afternoon tea will be in the small rose garden again. I will be giving walks through the gardens prior to that for anyone wishing to enjoy the sunshine and fine flowers in bloom this summer. Major, if I may beg your indulgence once again to aid me, I would be most appreciative."

"Your wish is my command, dear lady," replied the Major. Cassie was glad their easy relationship was still intact after her rejection of his offer.

Cassie opened a book she recently found in the library, tucked back in with other books of similar size and color. "This is something new for us, gentlemen. It was written by John Milton when he was losing his eyesight. I thought it would be of interest. The title is *On His Blindness.* *"When I consider how my light is spent...."*

The men leaned in to listen closely.

Afterwards, while getting ready for tea, Cassie kept glancing toward the manor house. She had stood up and sat down several times already when finally, she spotted what she had been waiting to see. She rushed forward holding out both hands, taking those of the pretty young woman with the bright golden ringlets tied up on both sides above her ears with a cute little hat perched between.

"Oh, Lady Cassandra, I am so glad you wrote. I do not know if I can keep my excitement down enough to follow your instructions, but I know you want the best for us so I will try to contain myself. I wore my favorite scent, and, no, it is not rose," the young woman said laughingly.

Turning to the older woman dressed in the London fashion of a few years ago, Cassie turned and welcomed her with a hug saying, "Oh, I have so missed you, Aunt Laura. So much has happened that I could not put into a letter. I hope to be home soon, at least for a short visit. As I wrote, the numbers of new patients are lessening, but so many need so much." She kissed that pleasant older lady on a powdery cheek.

Then Cassie turned toward the third woman in the group. "And this must be Lady Alice. Welcome, I am so glad you could make the trip," Cassie said warmly. "Please have a seat. Does everyone have their script? The gentlemen will be here anytime now. I know you'll enjoy meeting them."

Soon the men did arrive. They came in small groups as always, slowly, but not noticeably so. Somewhat like gentlemen taking a leisurely stroll with canes. Cassie smiled with pride as they entered the rose garden area with its marble benches and pillars holding urns full of greenery hanging over the edges. Major Bradley was there, of course, as well as the Sergeant. Most of Cassie's troops were finally present when she began.

"Gentlemen, I told you there was to be a surprise this afternoon. We have guests with us and I would like to introduce you to them." With that comment, some of the men became restless, but none of them left the group. Again, pride swelled in her breast for these men who had come so far since she had met them. She took none of the credit, but did take pleasure in their recovery and acceptance of their life.

"May I present Lady Stanton, my aunt."

With that introduction, Lady Stanton said loud enough for everyone to hear, "So glad to meet you all. I feel as if I know each of you. Cassie has written so much about you."

The gentlemen bowed their heads and some murmurings of, 'my lady' were heard.

Cassie continued, "Seated next to Lady Stanton is Lady Alice, a friend of my aunt."

Lady Alice, in a pretty alto voice, said, "I am so glad to meet you. I hope to speak with some of you more after tea."

Again, the gentlemen acknowledged the introduction.

"And finally, we have Miss Lucy Mason. She is a good neighbor from Littleton and Lieutenant Moore's betrothed." There was a murmur of surprised delight.

Christopher asked in amazement, "Lucy, you really came all this way? I, I have missed you terribly."

At that, Lucy jumped up from the bench and practically ran across the opening. Christopher must have heard her because he opened his arms to hold her close to his chest. The couple made quiet murmurings and walked off with their heads leaning closely together.

"I am sure we will all get to know Lucy a little more

after she and Ch, I mean, Lieutenant Moore, get through catching up," Cassie told the group, who were all smiling in understanding.

"While I pour, Lady Alice has agreed to read some original poetry as well as some of her favorites." Cassie nodded for that lady to proceed.

Lady Alice began in a well-modulated voice, the reading of some poignant poems about love, loss and regret. About being left behind and ignored and then forgotten. She held the attention of all present. Some men being moved to tears, discreetly hidden. When the last word was spoken, barely whispered because of such emotion, there was a slight silence and then enthusiastic applause from the appreciative audience.

"Major Bradley, would you mind escorting Lady Alice through the rose garden? I always find them so relaxing," Cassie requested.

The Major gave a slight bow and replied, "Certainly, it would be my pleasure, Miss Cassie." Then he held out his arm and waited for Lady Alice to place her hand on it saying, "Lady Alice, if I may?"

As Cassie refilled cups, Lady Stanton began a barrage of questions to each man present and started a lively debate, playing the devil's advocate. Cassie smiled with the love she felt for this wise, older lady. She felt in need of her counsel even if that counsel would consist of 'do what you feel is best for yourself'. Some of Lady Stanton's favorite words of advice.

Cassie was soon called to the pavilion where she found Lucy and Christopher sitting, a pile of belongings next to them.

"Oh, you're packed and ready to go home," she said enthusiastically. "I so hoped you would come to that decision, Christopher. There is no medical reason to stay and your mother will feel so much better for seeing you back home and safe once more."

"That is one of the main reasons and the other, of course, is to marry Lucy as soon as possible." Lucy blushed pink at his words, but the love that shown through her eyes for Christopher brought tears to Cassie's. "But mostly because I don't need to be here any longer. You have shown me there is a life for me back home. That I can learn to do most things I loved to do again. And that I am a man worthy of having a wife, children, and a good friend like you. Don't work yourself so hard and come home as soon as you can."

Cassie hugged each of them and wished them happy.

If Christopher and Lucy were getting ready to leave then that meant Aunt Laura was, too, and Cassie hadn't had any private time with her. Cassie caught up with her aunt on the way back to the drive at the front of the manor.

"I so wish for more time, but I know you want to reach the inn before nightfall. I appreciate you coming so much. Just by seeing you, I feel more in charge of myself, of my feelings," Cassie confessed.

"I know you are having a difficult time. I may be at fault, but please don't hold back on a relationship because you were raised by a hardened old spinster who never fell in love. It does not mean love is not out there for others, especially you." She patted Cassie's hand. "You were made for love and I should have recognized it much sooner than I did. Becoming a veterinarian was the beginning of accepting your loving nature. I should not have let you leave the London season as I did. By now you could have been a happily married woman with children to love and cherish."

"I'm glad you didn't," Cassie said honestly. "If you had, I would not have been called to help here and this is what I was born to do. I love and cherish these men and helping them to heal and return home has made me happy. I have my first graduates today and I feel that will bring many more to realize they, too, should begin the trip home. I only wish those empty beds were not filled so soon. I sometimes wonder if it will ever end," she finished in despair.

"My poor girl. You worry too much about others. Do not miss out on love, dear. Chase it if you must, but love is what life is all about. I would ask you to come home with me, right now, but I know you will not quit until all those beds are empty and every wounded man is healed and back with his family."

Her aunt gazed into Cassie's eyes trying to find the truth. "Please remember you will not be any help if you become too worn out. You seem thinner to me and although you say you are happy, I wonder if you know what that truly means." She finished with a hug and kiss on her niece's cheek. "Much love, darling. At least come for a visit,"

Christopher and Lucy joined them as they approached the coach Aunt Laura had rented for the trip.

"I see that Lady Alice has decided to stay the night as a guest of Lord Hedley," said Cassie. "I may end-up short by at least two patients after today." She smiled, hugging the young couple again before telling them to write her and the other gentlemen of the troop.

Cassie stood waving until the coach was out of sight. She smiled to herself as she turned, looking up to the second story to see the brooding man watching her.

Major Bradley approached Cassie appearing much as he had when she had first seen him. The black eye patch covering most of the damage to his face. He had foregone the darkened glasses that many of the blinded soldiers decided to wear. Cassie was unable to read his expression but stopped and waited for him to catch up with her where they would have some privacy.

He put out his hand and Cassie placed hers into it as she had become accustomed to doing. It formed a bond, a physical bond that represented the emotional one.

"I wanted to talk with you privately," he said.

"We are alone," she replied.

"How long have you known?"

"How long have I known you were a duke or how long have I known you loved Lady Alice?"

"How long have you been plotting?" he asked in a lighter note.

"Oh, I've been plotting ever since I can remember. I'm female you realize, don't you?" she teased.

"Either way, I owe you my life. I was in a bad humor when you came here but within a few days I was focusing less on myself and more on these less fortunate men. You made me feel ashamed for feeling sorry for myself, when I have so much and so many of these other men have so little. Now I owe you for giving me back the life I turned away from, for bringing me the woman I turned away from—all due to my own self-pity and foolishness."

"No, do not thank me. The work was yours. The change was yours and you always had Lady Alice. She was waiting for you to realize it. Her letter asking for news of your health and asking to help if she could, was what gave me the first bit of information on you. I wrote back and we have been in contact through the mails ever

127

since," Cassie confessed.

"My love for Alice was always present and I knew she would stand by me. She is honorable and loyal but…I couldn't stand knowing she remained out of pity. I turned back her letters and refused to acknowledge my family. I thought that would be enough to allow her to disregard our understanding. That she would find another gentleman with whom to share her life fully."

Cassie asked sardonically, "Are we speaking of the same Lady Alice who wrote all those lovely poems for you? Who worried and wept while you recovered yourself and your future?"

"I was a fool." Taking a deep breath, he continued, "I am extending an open invitation to come and stay with me and my duchess…" He paused. "How sweet those words…my duchess."

"I knew any man who loved his horse so much must be a romantic," she teased. "I'm so glad you realized what you have with Lady Alice."

He cleared his throat. "You are always welcome and my home is your home." He placed a chaste kiss on her surprised lips.

"Thank you, Duke or would you prefer, Major?" she asked now that his title was out in the open.

"Major, I think. I worked toward the rank and feel I have earned it. The other is a happenstance of birth. Lady Alice says you are a lady in your own right. Should I address you as such now?"

"No, I think it would put too great a gap between me and the men if they were to 'my lady' me all the day. I prefer simply Cassie to my friends." They walked arm in arm contentedly.

"Simply Cassie it is then." He agreed still smiling

and patting her hand.

"I will always cherish our friendship." Then changing the topic asked, "I take it you are returning home with Lady Alice?" At his agreement, she finished, "I will be waiting for the invitation to the wedding."

The next day was somber for the group under the pavilion. Cassie read the newspaper and tried to get the men to engage, but they were all feeling different stages of loss. Christopher and the Major were two of the original men in the group and their departure changed the dynamics more than Cassie realized.

Finally, frustrated by the lack of interest from the troops, she said with great emotion, "I know you are all thinking about Christopher and the Major leaving us and going home, but this is what you all have been working so hard to accomplish. Everything we do, everything we think about leads us to getting healed and going home. Taking up our lives as we left them if that is what we want or making a new life if that is the path for us. We should not see this as an end to anything. It is a birth of our freedom. Christopher and the Major are leading the way, holding the banner for the rest to follow."

She snapped the paper closed and stood. "Now, no more being melancholy. This is a celebration not a wake. Help me find an appropriate way to celebrate the next step in their lives and in a large way, the next step in ours," she said rallying the troops.

Men started to offer suggestions from getting drunk to dancing to singing and dancing with appropriate musical accompaniment. It was decided they would have a drummer and bagpiper pipe the two off the field of honor, so to speak. Then imbibing in a rum punch and a light meal eaten in the rose garden at midnight. That seemed to have broken the spell and the troops got back to normal and back to recovering.

# CHAPTER TEN

It had been raining for the past two days, not that it hadn't rained before. After all it was England, but these showers were accompanied by gusts of winds that blew cold rain in through the tent flaps, making everything damp and uncomfortable. The beds and much of the gear were moved into the east wing, lining the wide hallways.

The men were read to, the piano played for them yet they were still fretful. After a small argument over the outcome of a checkers game, Cassie suggested the two men arm wrestle to prove who was in the right. Not that it would, but it would keep them busy. Soon there were side bets being laid as to the winner and a couple of offers to wrestle the victor.

Cassie was standing over a table of men not interested in the wrestling or too wounded yet to participate. She emptied her small purse onto the tabletop and was explaining they needed to be able to recognize each coin by its size, weight or the design stamped into it. After learning that, they needed to make change for one another until they could do so without thinking about it. Explaining that unscrupulous vendors might try to cheat a blind person by returning incorrect change or counterfeit coin. They needed to be alert for such doings.

"Oh, Lord Hedley, do you have a three-shilling I might borrow? I find I am short a coin," she called out to that man.

Quinn entered the east hallway and went into the

men's parlor handing her the coin. "Lose a bet, Miss Woods?" he asked smiling, his gaze taking in her form, his nose her scent, his ears the music of her voice.

He tried not to sound too breathless or too happy to see her. After all, he kept away from her most of the time or timed his visits when there were others around. Many others so he wouldn't be tempted to take her into his arms and kiss her senseless.

It was little meetings as this one that kept him sane. Knowing he could find her when her draw became too strong, hear her voice reading to the troop or giving orders. He missed watching her from his upstairs windows during this rain and finally resorted to coming to the wing where he knew she would be.

"No, something the men needed to complete a project," she answered.

Bending she whispered into a young man's ear, "Permit me." She placed her hand lightly under his chin and lifted it to a proper level.

Quinn had seen her do this same motion before, but this time it seemed so intimate as she almost caressed the young soldier's face. The soldier immediately sat up straighter and held his head as Cassie raised it, sitting there as any sighted person would.

"I don't know about the other men, Miss Cassie, but I doubt I'll ever feel a sovereign again, let alone have to make change for one," said a newer soldier still wearing the bandages of war. A few others chuckled their agreement.

"Well, you never know so I don't want you cheated," she said as the table of men began fingering then passing around the coins.

Cassie turned toward Quinn and asked, "Is there

anything you needed or are you here for a visit?"

"I came to visit my dog. He used to keep me company on days like this when the rain seemed to never stop and it was too wet to go for a ride or even outside for a breath of fresh air," he confessed.

Cassie made a little snapping sound with her fingers and Rex was immediately at her side. He sat down quietly and she bent down and rubbed his ears thoroughly then cooed, "What a good boy you are. You are such a gem."

She stood and still smiling at Quinn said, "He is all yours for the rest of the day."

Quinn looked at his dog and realized what he had known all along. Rex had switched loyalties long ago. Hell, Quinn would have done almost anything Cassie wanted if she would rub him behind his ears.

Trying to dispel such thoughts he said, "Why don't I stay here and challenge you to a game of chess."

Cassie, always up for a challenge, smiled. "I accept." She palmed two pawns then held out both hands. "Call the hand."

They sat at the small table snugged up against the wall away from the others who were already occupied. Having selected white, Quinn took his first move, not really paying much attention to the board. Cassie took a moment to make her move then glanced up expectantly at him.

She smiled slyly and asked quietly, "What are you thinking about?"

"If that is your secret. Do you use the same tactics on the men as you did in training my dog? You make us all drool and fawn over your every word, your every touch?" Then Quinn made his second move.

"I think everything responds when there is true care and feelings behind the actions. Rex needed consistency of what was expected of him. He thrives being the pet of all these men and responds to their showering of affection," she explained as she too made a move on the board.

Quinn gave a derisive snort.

"Are you implying I could make you do things by merely scratching behind your ears or rubbing your belly till your hind leg jerked?" she asked smiling with mischief.

Quinn smiled at himself ruefully. "I'm going to have that image in my mind for the rest of the day. I won't be able to concentrate on anything but having you touching me."

He glanced up to find Cassie with a self-satisfied expression on her face. He felt the weight of defeat hovering over him as he asked, "I'm going to lose this game, aren't I?"

"Probably," she stated as she inched her bishop toward his queen.

It had only been two weeks since Christopher and the Major left Hedley Hall, but now the troops were diminishing at a faster rate than they were arriving. The doctor was taking more trips back to London and his wife. The footmen and valets were comfortable working with the blind and wounded men and now took the caring for them in stride, offering helpful advice that would be needed when the young men returned home. The entire staff all had one goal, to get these men ready for the world they needed to live in, the world they would have experienced if not for a stroke of fate. Cassie was beginning to feel her time at the manor was limited. With less to do, her thoughts turned to Quinn. How much she would miss him. How much she would regret not making more of the time here than she had. How much she ached to feel him next to her at night.

Could she put aside her ideas for women's freedom long enough to know what it was like to be in a man's arms? To find physical love without endangering her ideals? Her Aunt Laura had always taken her pleasure where she found it when she was younger. The lady thought nothing of doing so since she owed no one man her favors. Cassie had never felt she would be tempted to throw-over the stricter conventions governing a female's role. But why should men have the freedom to pursue who they wanted and desired while women were only allowed such freedom after they had presented their husband an heir and spare?

It wouldn't endanger her vows in the slightest. She wasn't right for Quinn, for any gentleman living in society. She wouldn't expect or accept any form of chivalry whether that came as a marriage proposal or a slip on the shoulder. She would remain her own person and leave when she was done. No recriminations and no perception of ownership.

Would it be so bad for Cassie to admit she desired more for herself? Wouldn't it be more like her taking an equal level of freedom to seek what she wanted? Who she wanted? Then walk-away with the knowledge and memory of a passionate night with a man she desired.

Cassie knew Quinn was already in his room. The valet had been sent away and was now sitting in the servants' quarters flirting up the pretty downstairs' maid. Cassie turned the door lever and slid into the room. Quinn was standing near the bed across the room in his shirtsleeves and peered over in a questioning way. When he realized who had come in, his face showed pleasure, but when Cassie reached behind her back and turned the key in the lock, his face showed surprised pleasure.

Cassie kept her gaze locked with Quinn's as he smiled suggestively and asked, "My pardon, Miss Woods, but did I miss an appointment? Was there something you wished to, umm, discuss with me?"

He took a step to the right as if to go towards her, she took a quick step to the left. He stopped and looked quizzically at her while continuing unhooking his cuff links. Cassie reached to her dress sleeve unbuttoning a sleeve at the wrist to leave it flutter open. Quinn's gaze was intently watching as she undid the small pearl buttons on the other wrist.

Raising his hands to his cravat, he began unwinding the still starched piece of fabric. Cassie removed the lace fichu tucked into her neckline and let it trail to the floor while Quinn's gaze fastened first on the piece of lace then on the newly exposed creamy neck. He took another step to the right and she took another to the left, keeping the same distance between them.

Quinn unbuttoned his shirtfront beginning at the top. Cassie, holding his gaze with her own, began slowly unbuttoning the front of her dress, one pearl button after another until it was open to below her breasts.

He seemed to catch his breath and a wide, welcoming smile, emphasizing his amazing dimples spread across his face as he strode two more steps to the right and turned the key in the doorway leading to his dressing room. Cassie mimicked his quick steps and now found herself next to the bed with Quinn standing between the two locked doors. A reversal of their original positions.

His gaze locked once more with Cassie's, and he said, "By my calculations, if we continue with this dance, I will be completely naked while you will still be unhappily clothed. Well, unhappily for me, that is. I am guessing that wasn't the plan?"

"I'm not sure I have a plan. Would you like to play 'lady's maid' and help me out of my dress?" she asked coyly.

"I'd be delighted to be of service." He cut across the room directly to Cassie's side. His gaze roamed over her face and a questioning expression met hers. He seemed to have made a decision and she knew she wasn't going to be happy with it.

"What exactly are you playing at, Cassie? This isn't you so what has you coming to a man's bedroom at night alone?"

"I thought we should finish what we started that night in the library."

"Yes, a very pleasant interlude, which I regret was interrupted. But perhaps that was best. Our emotions were too involved and I was under an erroneous opinion of your morals."

Neither of them touched the other. Cassie's hopes and feelings crushed. "Not willing to play lady's maid, I take it?"

He lifted his hands and began to button up the front of Cassie's dress much to her disappointment. She frowned and gazed down at the finished job then looked up into Quinn's eyes one last time.

"Well, I guess that puts me in my place." She took a deep breath. "I'm sorry to have kept you from your sleep," she finished and turned to leave before the full extent of her humiliation made itself felt.

Quinn, shaking his head slightly replied, "Not because I want you to leave, but because I must let you go to keep my sense of honor. I promised your aunt I would protect you while under my charge. I have already bent that line once with you. I want to be able to take you back to her and say I behaved honorably."

"With all due respect, my aunt would be the last one to insist on that promise. She raised me to be independent and to follow my own path. I thought that path led to you, but I was mistaken." She left his bedroom a wiser woman.

No one regretted having to turn Cassie away more than Quinn, but even a taste of what she was offering and he wouldn't be able to let her leave his bed. He wanted to throw something and break it but knew that wouldn't make anything feel better, not in the long run.

In the long run, he would need to go somewhere, anywhere, to take his mind off her and to keep his hands off her. Knowing she didn't belong to Moore, that she didn't belong to anyone, was playing havoc with his sleeping in the same house. He must find something that would call him away for a while until he could figure a way to keep him from enjoying her while enjoying her presence nearby in the tents.

The next morning, he told Nathan and Melanie he would go into the capital and speak with the officials in charge of getting pensions for wounded veterans. There must be funds or something these men could fall back on if they couldn't go back to whatever civilian job they worked at before the war, before their injuries.

Nathan offered to go with him, but Quinn told him to stay and be in charge of the Hall. The patients may need something and with both of them gone there would be no one to issue the orders. Quinn figured Melanie would accompany her husband to London if he went.

Quinn left riding on the big roan he always rode without telling anyone else he was leaving. He wasn't sure what to say to Cassie that wouldn't make it sound as if he was running away or make her feel she drove him from his own home. He hoped she didn't jump to that conclusion because it wasn't strictly true. He must leave to keep from behaving dishonorably to someone he had assumed protection over. He felt honor bound to return her as he found her—pure and innocent and kind.

Even if he once thought she was brought to Hedley Hall merely to be sent home with a bee in her bonnet after Lieutenant Moore told her what he thought of her, he now knew he had been wrong.

He couldn't figure out why he hadn't guessed she and Moore would never have made a couple. She was too wise, and funny and brave and Moore was too young. That pretty, little blond lady was much more the lieutenant's type and to find the girl actually moved in to take care of Moore's mother while he was in service was much more the type of girl the lieutenant needed and could handle. Someone more proper, more used to being biddable. Simply the opposite of Cassandra Wood.

Once in London, Lord Hedley went to the War Offices that sent him to the Quartermaster who sent him to Veterans Affairs and then Quinn took himself to Whites' to run down some retired military men. That is where he found the real truth. No one could help these men more than they could help themselves. There were so many men coming back wounded the government had run out of money way before they ran out of need and the wounded and maimed were still returning by the shiploads.

Quinn had a few home truths to unload on members of the House of Lords who he found at his club, but it seemed he was not the first to tell them that the country was mistreating their own war heroes. He didn't find any relief for the men or for his misery of missing Cassie. The trip was a total failure except for the fact he didn't bed a virgin under his protection in his own home. He took little comfort in the win.

Cassie was feeling restless, having fewer patients gave her more free time to think. She would be going home, probably before the end of summer. Certainly, before fall was over.

Should she go back to Aunt Laura? Although by the sounds of things from her letters, Aunt Laura had taken her own advice on grabbing love when you can and moved Ben in with her.

Cassie was certain he wasn't sleeping in the guest room. Well, good for them. It shows it's never too late. She could go to London and catch up with her friends from her come-out. Of course, most of them were married with a couple of children. Would she be happy there or would their lives taunt Cassie with might-of-been?

She asked to speak with Quinn after dinner. Quinn agreed, reluctantly. She would meet him in the library if that was acceptable after she ate her meal with the men. If he wished, he could keep her at Hedley Hall with him, but he would need to show some emotion towards her.

He was in a similar pose by the fireplace as the night

they first shared that passionate interlude. The one Quinn refused to repeat.

Cassie didn't wait for preliminaries. She had none, so stated, "I've decided to leave at the end of the week. That will give me time to make sure all the men are at a point where my leaving will not set them back in their recovery or learning." She stood there almost defiantly.

"You will be missed greatly by Dr. Landon and the troops. Are you sure this is what you wish to do?" he asked casually.

She stated bluntly making him know he was responsible for her leaving, "Why do you bother asking? You won't even notice I'm gone. You ignore me most of the days I am here."Color washed into Quinn's face as he held his hands to his side in fists. "Do I ignore you when I try to sleep at night wishing I could feel your hair spread across my pillow? When I stay awake dreaming of having your breasts pressed against my naked chest? The taste of your mouth lingering on mine till I can't think straight? Do I ignore you when I hold myself back from going to your room, taking you in my arms, and crushing my pelvis to yours? Do I ignore you when I ache so badly to feel me enter you, making you part of my body in the most intimate way possible? Is that when I ignore you?"

"I don't understand. Why didn't you say something? Why did you keep pushing me away? I came to you.…" Her mind raced with these images, these confessions which were so close to her own wants and wishes.

"Because my sweet, dear Cassie is that you only came to me after a loss and you were seeking comfort. I couldn't take advantage of your feelings for others. I know this has been difficult on you. I took you out of a very good life and I brought you here to see the cruelest things man does to man. I should have sent you away, but I was selfish and kept you here. I should have been stronger, but I couldn't face not being able to see you. I couldn't admit what you meant to me. But truly—I never ignored you."

Cassie stood quietly thinking. Was Quinn, right? Did she only come to him for comfort over a loss or for relief from the constant strain of being strong for the men? She peeked at him. "I'm sorry if you felt I was using you. I didn't realize the situation through your eyes. Again, I apologize for keeping you from your sleep." She turned to leave.

Quinn reached out preventing her movements. "Did you listen to what I said? I didn't mind being used by you. I wanted to lessen some of your worry. I wanted to help lift some of the burden, but I am only human. I also wanted you so badly I almost broke with my own moral code." Softly he said, "This may kill me, but come here."

He folded her into his arms bringing his head down to cover her trembling lips with his own firm mouth.

The kisses they shared were tokens of forgiveness and absolution. They were a remedy for healing hearts, if not broken, then at least badly bruised by the events of the past months. Tears were still glistening in her eyes when Quinn pulled away and handed her a clean handkerchief.

"I better let you get to sleep. I agree going home is for the best until you know your own mind."

Cassie merely nodded and slowly walked out the library door.

Quinn turned toward the table of decanters thinking that was the hardest thing he had ever done, but it was the best for Cassie. He needed to know that she was his because she wanted to be and not due to feeling lost now the troops were not in need of her as much.

When time eased her emotions, when her aunt's support rebuilt her strength, when she could think of her time here in Hedley Hall with more joy than pain, he hoped she would return to him. Let him know when the time was right for them to pursue what he knew was between them.

He knew he was taking a chance at allowing her to leave him. He wasn't aware of a man in Littleton she could end-up accepting in her weakened condition, but no one wrote to her and Moore never indicated there was competition from that front.

No matter, she needed time to recover and he would have to wait that time out. No matter how long it took or how difficult he found it.

# CHAPTER ELEVEN

Cassie was welcomed home by the whole village, it seemed. Everyone owned a pet or sheep or pig they wanted her to check on. But after the first two weeks and meeting every batch of kittens and pups born while she was away, and every flock of every kind of farm animal there was, the house calls quieted down.

She knew her neighbors were interested in her experience at Hedley Hall. After all, Christopher, Lucy and even Christopher's mother sang her praises. Giving her credit for saving Christopher's life, his marriage and even his mother's life.

Trying to explain she hadn't done that much or trying to share the credit with Dr. Landon, didn't work. The locals all shook their heads and said what a modest heroine she was. But they knew she was beyond gold and took pride in her being their neighbor.

The animals were Cassie's eventual salvation. They had no expectations besides taking comfort in her care of them, her constant worrying over their health and well-being. She aided a stray in giving birth to a large batch of puppies so she found herself helping to feed the smallest of the litter. The mother had been neglected prior to being dropped off in the village. Just another orphan that would soon call Aunt Laura's cottage home, too.

Then there was the bunny the barn cat got hold of, but didn't have time to kill before it was rescued by the children of the cat's owner. They brought it to her, the little girl with tears welling in her eyes as she offered the furry little body up to Cassie in both hands and tearfully asked that she save it.

Cassie didn't have the heart to explain that if they saved it and let it go free, it would probably make its home in the girl's father's garden. Then he would have to shoot it and they would have it for supper one night. The thought went through her mind, of course, but she couldn't explain the truth of life to a child sympathetic enough to try to save the life of an injured hare.

Cassie finally felt she was returning to normal. She no longer startled awake worrying about the new patient who appeared as if his limb was turning gangrenous or the one who became despondent after hearing his mother died waiting for him to come home.

The worries and nightmares of a country veterinarian were nothing compared to those who cared for the wounded and Cassie was grateful of that fact. Taking comfort that the war was indeed over and all the injured men brought home. That fact lessened any guilt she felt at leaving Hedley Hall since most of her troop were recovered enough to return home.

Now Cassie confronted her own demons and healed her heart after foolishly falling in love with an honorable man. Every night she thought about how she could have handled things differently with Quinn. Accepted his need to remain aloof to keep the proprieties. Understand his need to uphold the gentleman's obligation to guard any woman under his protection. She knew she was to blame for their uncomfortable parting.

A parting that didn't change the facts. Cassie would never be a countess. She may have been raised learning all the right things a countess needed to know, but she would never accept the life of a titled man's wife. The limited endeavors allowed them. The constant visits to one another's home for tea or luncheon or dinner. Living vicariously through their husbands or, if they were blessed, through their children. Cassie, like her aunt, had disavowed ever becoming one of those women.

Aunt Laura made a trip out to the garden as Cassie cultivated the plants she used in her medicinal remedies. Sitting on the nearby bench, she commented on how nice the garden appeared and how lovely the fall weather was and how warm the day for the time of year.

Narrowing her eyes, Cassie asked, "What exactly is it you find so difficult to say to me, Aunt Laura? You've never felt the need to prevaricate before."

"I know my dear, and I feel silly, well down right foolish having to say it now, but I think I wish to be married." As Cassie's mouth dropped open her aunt continued, "I know, I know. I've not been a supporter of the married life. At least not for the woman. After all, it seems like we get the short end of the deal." She blushed rosily at how that sounded. "But actually, I find I now like the idea of being part of a couple. Belonging to someone who isn't a blood relative, someone who chose me out of all the other women who could have been chosen. Do you understand, my dear?" her aunt asked as if she wasn't sure she herself did.

"You love Ben. It's understandable, of course, and I think it the grandest idea for you two. You belong together and being married in a church lets everyone else know as well. No one will be able to separate you for any reason, none what so ever and I concur. You and Ben should marry." Then she went on with the transferring of small plants into trays to keep in the greenhouse over the winter for replanting in the spring. "Have you decided on a date? I was thinking of my moving into the little cottage nearer town and…"

"Cassandra Woods, you will do no such thing. We are still family and you have been here with Ben and me and it has all worked out fine. I don't expect you to leave me because I'm changing my last name. After all, I'm still your aunt and now Ben will be your uncle. We never even thought our getting married would mean changing anything around here. Ben will back out if he thought you meant to leave us."

"I don't wish to intrude, even if you and Ben have been toge…, I mean, have known each other for so long. A newly married couple should have time alone," argued Cassie.

"Heavens, we are past the alone stage, my dear. Ben is glad we're past the climbing out the upstairs window stage." Aunt Laura laughed at Cassie's wide-eyed shock.

Swallowing the lump in her throat that formed thinking of the elderly Ben hanging from the second floor as he snuck out of the upstairs' bedroom, she said, "Aunt Laura that sounds dangerous even for a young man. What if he had fallen and broken something?"

"Then we would have had to wake you up to put him back together and I might have decided to marry him a whole lot sooner. When you left, I realized what my life would be like when you marry." She gave Cassie a hard glare. "And my dear child, you will marry no matter what you think right now. You were made for marriage and a loving husband and having your own children. I thought that life was never for me. I absolutely knew it. I made you think you were exactly like me. I didn't mean to do so, I assure you."

The woman who was as a mother looked out over the garden before continuing, "My plans for my life were just that, my plans. I felt you should have the freedom to make your own, but that wasn't necessarily to follow my path. Can't you see how different we are? We get along together, but we are definitely not two peas in a pod. I've failed you if I didn't instill that in you from the very first summer you visited me." The older woman seemed very concerned.

"I know, Aunt Laura, and really, I'm not trying to emulate you. I do enjoy the freedom my life has now, but the other, the married kind of life has its attractions, too. I haven't found a way of making that happen, yet, is all. I may find someone who appreciates me for myself and won't think I'm too much a hoyden to be a married lady at the same time. Meanwhile, you will see me at the breakfast table." Cassie tried to make her aunt know all was well and she would stay living in the cottage as she always had.

The wedding of Lady Stanton to plain Mr. Ben Green was the talk of the village. Some saying they knew there was something between them all along while others insisting Ben placed the woman on a pedestal and would never have thought to even say her name without permission. Either way, they all seemed happy the two older people were getting married and a party was to be held in the rectory after the service.

Ben wore his best suit but bought new shoes and cravat for the occasion. Lady Stanton, soon to be Mrs. Green, was wearing a dress she owned since her come-out in London. It had gone through the same dinners, balls and outings that Cassie went through twenty years later.

As Cassie was straightening the veil, she became aware that Aunt Laura wasn't really that old at all. She was only two and twenty years older than Cassie, making her less than four and forty years old now. And Ben, although grey and having a few wrinkles around his eyes and the hair thinning on top of his head, was less than fifty. That wasn't so old. In fact, many men that age were having young families. She looked speculatively at her aunt and smiled, maybe there was time for Cassie to manage all she wished for, too.

Cassie returned home with her aunt's veil and a few other items left at the church when the two newlyweds left on honeymoon. She spent several days alone in the cottage, mentally thanking her aunt for not allowing her to move into one of her own. Cassie found she didn't like the solitary life of a spinster after all and missed even the little bit of society the couple in love shared with her.

That momentous wedding started a slew of weddings and engagements, as if spring was in the air. Christopher and Lucy were the next couple to be married having called the banns even before Aunt Laura and Ben. But Lucy and Christopher's mothers made so many plans waiting for him to come home from the war they wanted to get them all implemented which took time. Time to make arrangements for his fellow officers to be free to attend. For the dressmaker to get the mothers' gowns done and fitted to everyone's satisfaction. For Lucy's dress to be sewn and delivered from London. To make sure the perfect flowers were delivered and placed in the church and in the country manor where the wedding breakfast would be held. And to collect the white doves Lucy felt were essential to showing how much they loved one another and that as the doves, their love would soar.

Christopher confided in Cassie once when she was there to lend her support with whatever needed to be done. "When I left Hedley Hall, I was so excited and so sure about marrying Lucy. Now after all these weeks I'm afraid of letting her down. You know, on the wedding night."

Knowing he had no close male family member or friend in the area, she wasn't surprised at this confidence. Cassie accepted what he said as a medical person and answered as honestly as she could without having any real experience.

"None of your injuries will prevent you from being the man Lucy is expecting or needing on her wedding night. You are thoughtful and kind and I know you love her. I know Lucy will be nervous and feeling she isn't as prepared as she should be. That is quite natural, too, and you must assure her that you will be content no matter what happens that night. And you will be fine, both of you. Lucy has asked me enough questions and I have reassured her that she will be safe with you."

At Christopher's furled brow, Cassie continued, "She asked if she should let you know it would be all right to forgo those sorts of relationships if you wanted. Lucy feared you may not be able to, umm, perform as a husband after your injury. That perhaps that was why you didn't ask for her in the first place."

"You know why I didn't…."

Cassie touched his arm. "I assured her you were all man and you merely wanted to save her from seeing the ravages of war that surrounded you there at the manor."

They stood together awkwardly and she finally asked a little hesitantly, "Do you need me to explain anything? I mean, answer any questions?"

"Good God, Cassie, I know what to do. It's just that we've never been together that way and I'm a little nervous. As you said, Lucy seems a little anxious, but if you say it will be fine, then it will be," he ended firmly.

"I didn't mean to indicate you didn't know what to do. I know you hadn't before you left for the service, before I left for the London season anyways," she said in defense. Unintentionally reminding him of how close they once were about everything, even something so personal.

"You are right, as usual, but in the army, you hear things. Then one night after a little drinking and a little flirting you find yourself alone with the serving wench from the pub and then she teaches you a few things. I guess that's how one learns such things isn't it?" he asked embarrassed, even though he was trying to act as if he had sangfroid.

"Yes, Christopher, I think that is exactly how it is done even if it may not be the best way. Lucy won't have anyone to judge you against so how you treat her will set the pace for the rest of your marriage. I know you'll make sure it is the right way," Cassie said, glad the conversation was at an end and glad she hadn't had to have a similar one with her aunt or Ben before their wedding.

The day of the young couple's wedding was bright and clear if a little chilly but no one seemed to mind. They were all out to see the wedding of the county occur the same as they had two weeks earlier for Ben and Laura. Lucy's sister stood up beside her and one of Christopher's fellow officers stood beside him. The Reverend again officiated and the church was again packed as everyone wanted to wish the young couple the best.

The wedding breakfast was immense by local standards and the musicians brought in were going to be spoken about for months if not years as the best orchestra the villagers ever had the privilege of hearing. Cassie only had to remember the tiny group of musicians in her troops to know any music can be the most wonderful when played at the right moment.

Since the young couple didn't wish to leave Christopher's mother alone, they were planning on staying at the Moore home, larger than most but nowhere as large as Hedley Hall. The locals would give them a week or two alone before they began issuing invitations to homes for dinner and small gatherings. The locals accepted Christopher, handicap and all, back into their open arms and now the couple was the elite of the county and wouldn't be left to rest idly at home whether they were newlyweds or not.

# CHAPTER TWELVE

Lady Cassandra Woods was back where she swore, she would never be again. The Duke of Winterset had married his most beautiful fiancée, Lady Alice Waters, and half of London was in his ballroom in celebration. Cassie, wearing a dress from her come-out that still appeared as fresh and lovely as it had when she first wore it, peered around at the other ladies swirling about the room and felt she hadn't embarrassed the Duke and Duchess.

She was glad she allowed the borrowed lady's maid to pile her hair in curls and weave pearls and silk ribbon through it. She must admit for a spinster she looked pretty good and many of the men present thought so too, although their interest might not have been of the purest intent. Her aunt's reputation for women's rights was well known among the ton.

Cassie spent most of her time with the disabled veterans she helped while at Hedley Hall, so was busy catching up with how they were doing fitting into their old lives or making new ones. Some married sweethearts who had waited for them, others began new careers or re-evaluated their relationships with family members. They spoke openly about these things around the table with men who would understand and were used to adding in their opinions or helpful suggestions as they had when they were in the tents and part of Cassie's Troops.

The Major danced with Cassie to many guests'

wonderment since there were many ladies of higher rank there. He walked her onto the dance floor after having the first waltz with his new Duchess. He was even more confident and impressive after being home and taking charge of his lands and houses than he had been at the manor.

They spoke about Triumph and the several foals expected in a few months. Not exactly what most couples speak of while dancing to a romantic waltz, but then the Major and Cassie always had an unusual connection. Forged during a time when both were going through a change in their lives. She knew the man—his soul and he knew hers in a way few people do who are not intimate. She missed his bright mind and sense of humor but not as much as she missed the man who had been their host.

There was less time for Cassie to speak with Alice being the bride and in great demand by the guests. But since they wrote regularly, it wasn't as important. She might even make arrangements to come into London to meet with her friend after Alice and the Major returned from their wedding trip to the wilds of Whales.

Seeing Alice's bright smile and the unconditional love between the newly married couple, Cassie knew she had done the right thing bringing Alice to the rose garden in that secretive manner.

Several men not known to Cassie appeared asking for a dance, which she accepted, or a walk in the famous gardens, which she refused. She was on edge at first dreading while at the same time looking forward to her first meeting with Quinn after that last fateful discussion at the hall. She really thought she would go back to finish working with the wounded men, but Dr. Landon wrote informing her he felt he could do more good in London and so was disbanding the temporary hospital at Hedley Hall.

Melanie wrote the men were taken to a boardinghouse outside London that Quinn purchased and were being housed there. The staff were using the area to help the newly blinded find their way around the big city and use their skills in new ways. Setting them up with jobs and living quarters so they could become independent. Her heart swelled with pride at the men's growth and at Quinn's generosity.

Then he was there, like the waters parting for Moses, the crowded dance floor formed a kind of funnel with Quinn, wearing the de rigueur evening clothes and appearing devastatingly handsome, at its apex. Cassie tried to turn away as if their gazes had not met, but knew the moment he started towards her. She glanced around for an escape, but then remained in her chair, waiting for the inevitable.

"Miss Woods, how lovely you look. If I didn't know better, I would think you were part of this scene every night of the year." He smiled but the smile didn't go as far as his eyes.

"Yes, Lord Hedley, it was very kind of Lady Alice, I mean, the Duchess, to remember me. I wasn't aware she would deem me sufficiently acceptable for this honor. But it was good to talk with some of the men and I'm sure that is why she did it," Cassie told him, explaining why a non-ton as he thought her, would be sitting in the middle of one of the most influential events of the year.

"Yes, I thought I recognized most of these uniformed men. At times, it seems like so long ago." He seemed to be thinking back almost half a year to before they met.

"The Major was very generous." She felt she must say something to keep from remembering, to keep from hearing his apologies about kissing her. She was sure he was trying to let her down easily. "The Duke sent tailors to make clothes for those who didn't have the means to get them for this evening as well as offering transportation. It was very thoughtful of him."

"Yes, it has never been said the Duke didn't take care of his troops, or in this instance, Cassie's Troops." This time the smile did enter his eyes.

"No matter what else I do or where I go, I'll probably be most proud of those weeks at the hall and meeting those men. It made me question my life as I helped them return to theirs," she said without thinking to whom she spoke.

Quinn watched her closely and spoke crossly. "Then if you had it to do all over again, you'd do it the same way? I mean, from what I could see, this could have been all yours. The Duke gave you a bona fide offer and all you had to do was say, yes."

Cassie narrowed her eyes, trying to find the man she thought she cared so much for, but he wasn't there with them tonight. She said sadly, for her loss, "The Major was taking the easy way out. Going after someone who didn't have a measuring rod for what he had been to what he was at that moment. I was his way out, to not return to his potential, his fate. If he hadn't figured it out that evening, then he would have soon enough."

Quinn watched her, seemingly trying to form a question. "Is this what you truly feel or are you telling me what you think I want to hear?"

She felt the need to interrupt this discussion before

it became too personal. "I'm sorry, but I'm being called away. Please give my best to Colonel Lancaster and Lady Melanie. I know they didn't wish to travel this close to her confinement."

Cassie didn't want to hide the fact she and Melanie wrote each other regularly since he probably franked the letters. "It was so nice reminiscing with you." Then she was up and gone in a flurry of cream-colored silk and rhinestones.

The rest of the evening was spent making sure Quinn wasn't already in any room she entered or close to where she sat hidden among the potted palms and Ficus.

Finally, after midnight, Cassie, Aunt Laura, and her newly married husband, Ben, returned to the hotel where they would spend the rest of the night and return to Littleton in the morning.

As Cassie predicted, Aunt Laura and Ben were as bad as turtle doves cooing at each other all day, but they never made her feel as if she were in the way. They continued as they always had and Cassie was glad, they were so happy together. It made her wonder what Quinn was doing and if his life was back to normal, as well.

Cassie went over the time they spoke at the wedding for the duke and duchess and thought how Quinn hadn't seemed to be himself. He seemed to be holding something back and she realized so had she. Instead of extending a welcome, she withdrew and acted as if they were mere acquaintances meeting at an event. She not only didn't speak of their past, she refused to allow him to either.

She should have taken Quinn somewhere private, somewhere they could finish with one another or at least offer a reason why things had ended so abruptly. Only she was a coward. Afraid of what he would say, the words he might use to cut her to the quick so she kept their conversation away from the past. Instead acting as if she was happy to be there without an escort, enjoyed living with a set of newlyweds, was content being the spinster veterinarian of Littleton.

Rather than two people who were such a significant part of initiating the event, they spoke as strangers. The slightest difference could have the wedding they were attending never occurring. Things could have been so different—for them all.

If Quinn hadn't come for her in the first place, if she hadn't seen the need for her help with the wounded soldiers, if she hadn't remained at Hedley Hall. So much would have been altered, so many lives changed and not for the better.

She tried to remember everything he had said. How he held his head, his hands and then she thought back and knew his hands were clenched at his sides, his elbows stiff so as not to reach for her. Not to enfold her in his arms? Had he been about to ask her to dance when she made up the excuse to leave him standing alone at the edge of the dance floor? What had she been thinking?

She knew what she had been thinking or rather what she had been afraid of. She was afraid he would once again rebuff her, set her aside with small words about not wanting to take advantage of her emotions for others, turn her away from his body when she wanted most to hold tightly to him.

If she rode to Hedley Hall right now would he welcome her or find some other proper way to fob her off once again? Would he even be there or would he be in London for the season until the holiday drove him back to his family? Would London have been where he normally stayed if the troops hadn't been housed in his home, his brother newly back from the war and injured?

Melanie slipped a few sentences about Quinn into every letter and Cassie knew she read and re-read those parts as if every word meant something more than what it said. But Melanie didn't say he was pining or morose or any of the things Cassie would expect him to be if he loved her or even desired her as she did him. Of course, no one would think she was either of those things, but she was, at least inside.

She was very, very much pining for Quinn—his grey eyes, his crooked grin and his dimples. She never thought about a man's dimples as much as she did Quinn's. If he had ever taken her up on any of her offers of more, she would have those memories, too. The man was too honorable or too kind to let her know he didn't have those sorts of feelings for her.

But there had been those kisses. Those wonderful, heat filled kisses. No, a man cannot feign that Cassie was sure. He had to desire her to some extent, but he wasn't going to pursue her honorably. He didn't follow up on her offer. Again, honor getting between the two of them.

# CHAPTER THIRTEEN

Cassie was in the work shed, making a list of plants and herbs she needed for the medicines she liked to keep on hand, when she felt someone watching her. Glancing up, expecting a neighbor to have her check on a sick animal, she found the piercing grey eyes of the man who was never far from her thoughts.

"I wrote your father for permission to marry you."

Not wanting to sound as breathless as she felt, she asked as if the answer didn't mean the world to her, "And what did he have to say?"

"Firstly, he asked if I was sure I had the right man. Next, if I had the honor of winning your hand and your heart, then he had no objections. That you were your own woman and he trusted in your judgement." His eyes seemed to plead with her. "Have I? Won your heart because you have had mine since you left my home. I thought we would be able to come together at the duke's wedding. That we could put the horror of war and brutality behind us. Meet as equals beginning over. A fresh start to what I hoped would be forever."

"I, ah, I…" What could she say? How could she respond when she had crushed whatever there was between them? How she worried that she would lose herself if she allowed him to win? But was that really the case? She had to be honest. Not only with him but with herself.

"I feared I would let you down. We don't live in the same world. Not the real world. At Hedley Hall I could forget everything and be me. If I stayed, when things returned to normal you would expect a normal countess of me. I know what that means and I know I will come up wanting."

"My dearest, my darling, I know who you are. More than I would ever have known by only seeing you in society or at balls. I loved everything about you – except the part of thinking you belonged to another man. That you were promised to another man whether you had broken that engagement or not."

"You thought less of me but still wanted me?"

"I think my initial reaction to you was originally lust when we met in the brush alongside the road. Once I found you to be the woman I was seeking, I berated myself for not disliking you. Angry that my feelings for you rejoiced in the idea you had jilted a wounded soldier. I wasn't very pleased with myself."

"I could tell. You seemed to take it out on me."

"If only you knew how strongly I felt. Perhaps you would have soothed my brow as you had others'.

"Not much has changed, my lord. I'm still working with animals and digging in the garden. Not accomplishments of a countess."

"I don't care what you do with your time as long as at the end of the day you return to me. I don't care if you befriend my servants and beguile my stable staff. That you are on a first name basis with every four-legged stock animal in my tenants' sheds. I want you, Cassie, as my wife. The mother to my children."

She remained frozen to the ground. How easily he made it seem to accept. That he seemed to know her and accept her with all her differences than why should she hold his life against him? He seemed more than willing to give her the freedom she needed.

"Did you miss me, Cassie?" he asked bluntly. "Am I welcome?" A worried expression crossed his face.

"Yes. And yes. Why did it take you so long to come for me?" she asked quietly as she walked to him and was enfolded in his arms.

"I wanted to give you time to know yourself again but I couldn't wait any longer. I wasn't sure you would want me but I knew I must find out. Then try to change your mind if it wasn't made up in my favor." He smiled into her upturned face.

"I always knew. You were the one with the doubts."

"Never about my feelings for you, woman." He covered her mouth with his lips. Kissing and nipping the lower lip until she opened and accepted the adoration he gave.

After several minutes, Quinn took a step back straightening his clothes. "I have to attend to serious matters so no more of that." He finished the sentence with a quick kiss on Cassie's pouty lips.

"Cassandra Woods, will you do me the honor of becoming my wife?" he asked pointedly.

"No throwing yourself prostrate on the ground begging me? No chest pounding declaring your undying adulation?" Then more quietly, almost a whisper, "No saying that you love me?"

"Yes, to all of those. It goes without saying but if you need the words, I will be glad to make that my goal in life." Then said seriously, "I am begging you to put me out of my misery and marry me. I will pound my chest in adulation of you and your beautiful body. And it goes without saying I love you and cannot even think of not having you in my life."

Then he confessed, "I've been miserable since you left Hadley Hall. I will stay here, live in this shed if I must, until you agree to marry me. Tell me we can do all those things with each other that have kept me awake every night since you left me."

"We have had the same dreams. I love you and will marry you without hesitation." Smiling her Mona Lisa smile, she pulled him close to her once again.

That evening over dinner, Quinn explained to Cassie that he had brought a special license with him. "I have already spoken with the local rector to see if he would marry us as soon as possible. I explained everything to your Aunt Laura and Ben earlier that I was here to propose and hoped you would accept me."

Aunt Laura added, "I had no doubt and told Quinn he must stay with us till the wedding since we have an empty guest room."

Quinn said, "I accepted because it will keep me close to Cassie so she wouldn't talk herself out of marrying me."

The next morning, the small wedding she planned on was attended by everyone in the village. Word travelled quickly and everyone wanted to see the man who had, for a second time, stolen her from them.

Most of the attendees explained to her that once they saw how in love the two of them were, they forgave Lord Hedley for wanting her with him. After all, the minister explained, a couple that much in love didn't have a chance of not being together. It seemed as if the entire town wished her happy as Cassie and her new husband climbed into his carriage and once again headed to Hedley Hall.

Part way through the trip, fuming impotently, Quinn

complained. "This is a damn long ride home."

"We could kiss."

"No, we can't. I'm having a hard-enough time holding onto my control as it is. Having you rub up against me every time we hit a bump is excruciating and there are too many damn bumps for my peace of mind."

She could tell he was getting more bad-tempered by the minute.

"What can I do? Is there something I can do to make you feel better?" she asked innocently.

"Yes. Stop being so obliging. I won't have our first time together as man and wife in a moving carriage. Snuggle against me." At her hesitation he added, "I know what I said, but I'm just grumpy from not getting any sleep the last couple of weeks."

He pulled her closer to him. His hand slid to the side of her breast and he seemed to be content with that much latitude. She was surprised at how it seemed to calm him. He spent the rest of the trip telling her how happy he would make her and the trips they would take together and the children he was hoping to give her.

And the best part, Nathan and Melanie had gone for an extended visit to Melanie's parents' home until after the baby was born, perhaps longer.

They would be alone at Hedley Hall. Something that had never happened before.

Milton stood at the door and there was barely time to utter a welcome home when Quinn carried his bride past the opened-mouth butler and up the curved stairway.

He laid her on the still made bed as if she were a precious parcel saying, "There you are, Lady Hedley, exactly where I want you for at least the next two, no make that, four days. I don't know if that will satisfy our need, but it should give us a good start. I don't want to be known as one of those men who ignore their wives or rush through things."

Cassie laughed as she took off her hat and threw it on a nearby chair. "I don't think I'm going to feel ignored," she said smiling. "I remember the talk between us in the carriage and all the things you told me you would like to do with me."

He watched her take out a few hairpins and shake out the tresses as they shimmered and straightened down her back. Then shaking himself, began shrugging out of his coat and waistcoat throwing them towards a sofa near the fireplace. As he removed the cufflinks, he looked up to see Cassie starting to unbutton the tight sleeves at her wrists.

Facing her, he slowly unbuttoned his shirt having dispelled with the cravat already. Cassie turned her body toward him and unbuttoned the tiny pearl buttons down the front that made up the only adornment to her dress. Pulling his shirt over his head, he sent it in the direction of his coat.

Cassie started to raise herself enough to get the dress over her head when she heard a low growl from her husband as he declared, "Enough of this teasing. I am going mad not touching you. Let me help you get this off and we can worry about the other later. I always knew I was at a disadvantage with this strip tease." With that realization, he smiled a dazzling smile, which showed off his dimples to her great glee.

Then he joined her on the bed. Cassie with only her stockings and chemise left while Quinn wore his breeches and stockings. He evidently told her the truth when he said he couldn't wait any longer and laid her back kissing her neck and nuzzling into her hair spread across the pillow.

With his fingers, he petted and caressed the tresses as if he had never felt anything so fine. Kissing her mouth, he was welcomed into it as she had always offered herself up for him. It seemed as if he could never get enough of her sweetness.

He released her lips so he could remove the chemise that was frustrating him. Then covered her body as he dreamt of doing for months. Her bare breast against his bare chest was as exhilarating as he knew it would be. He unconsciously ground his pelvis against her and felt her rubbing against him in return.

That almost killed him. Did she know what she was doing or was this a natural response to his needs and movements? He didn't care, he loved everything she was doing. Loved every motion, every curve and bump.

Quinn's hands roamed Cassie's entire body. Brushing over the most intimate area knowing if he paid too much homage there, he wouldn't do right by Cassie and this night was all about her. He had promised himself and took a vow to make this special, as special as he felt being allowed access to her body.

His hands encountered the stockings and he bent to roll them off her delicate feet and tossed them toward his clothing. Gazing back over his bride, his mouth went dry and he would have sworn he stopped breathing entirely. He gazed into Cassie's eyes and saw she was watching him, watching his enthralled attention as he let himself take in the glory that was her woman's body and showing the enjoyment he felt doing so.

Cassie's breath hitched as Quinn's hands wandered over her skin. Not even when bathing had she ever touched herself in such a manner and was mesmerized by the expression on Quinn's face. Adoration? It humbled her to think this man who she loved so fiercely loved her in return and to the same degree.

She watched as he raised himself to remove his breeches and return to her side. Instead of kissing her lips, he bent his head and suckled one breast. Cassie arched into his mouth seeking something but wasn't sure what. She felt calmer when Quinn's hand covered, then rubbed, the other breast.

Cassie heard of this phenomenon, but to have muscles and she knew not what else, contract upon Quinn's suckling and kissing her breasts was incredible. Cassie wasn't sure what she was supposed to do in reciprocation, but felt she must touch Quinn in some way. Driven to feel the well-muscled chest, his nipples pebbling beneath her searching fingers and the feel of the hair lightly covering this newly discovered playground.

Starting to writhe beneath Quinn's administrations, Cassie began to chant, "Enter me, Quinn. Please come to me."

Quinn almost broke.

Leaving off his attentions to her breasts, he whispered between kisses, kisses on her neck, above her breasts and under her ears, trying to calm himself into being able to take his bride with the care and love he promised himself he would use.

Bowing to Cassie's pleas, Quinn lowered his mouth to her breasts as he let his hand cover her Venus mound then slid a finger into the moist warmth between her legs. It was almost his undoing. He mimicked the movement he dreamt for weeks of doing to her with his body. Cassie seemed to quiet as she realized this was what she desired without knowing it. Then that wasn't enough for her either and she began the chant again, trying to reach a pinnacle she didn't have a concept of yet.

Quinn argued with himself about whether to bring Cassie to her peak before entering her or get her prepared for him, but wait to have her climax when he entered her. It was a damn difficult decision and one he thought he would have made by now, by some sort of divine spirit who would guide him through this with her. The best way for them. He didn't want to get it wrong.

Cassie begged again, "Please, Quinn, join with me. Enter me."

That was as much as Quinn could take and said quietly, "I'll stop if you need me to. This might hurt, but then I plan to make it better. Trust me?"

"I've always trusted you," she whispered.

And with that, Quinn moved over his trusting wife placing his knee between her legs to make room for his body. Cassie realized the need and separated her legs giving him full access to the most intimate part of her body with the most intimate of his. He hesitated at the entrance, but Cassie was having none of that and thrust her pelvic up and toward him.

Quinn felt the internal resistance then Cassie thrust again and he found himself sheathed completely. He waited for a denial from her, but not hearing any, he began the age-old rhythm. Cassie was moving her head back and forth, her hands gripping and pulling his hips closer to her until he felt her muscles tense and throb against his appendage. He was spiraling with his wife to a most earth-shattering release as his seed filled her womb.

They lay in the bed enjoying the aftermath of their intense lovemaking and Cassie, rubbing Quinn's chest said, "That was the most glorious experience I've ever felt. Thank you, my lord, for giving it to me." She kissed him on the mouth.

"My pleasure, my lady." And he kissed her in return. "Tell me something. When you call me, my lord, what are you really saying to me?"

Cassie gave that little Mona Lisa smile and admitted, "At first it was short for 'my lord and master' since I found you rather bossy and possibly a little too full of yourself. After I knew you better, it was my way of saying, my love."

Quinn feeling so over-whelmed with emotion began the entire love making process all over again.

## A word about the author...

A voracious reader her whole life, author Susan Payne loves the written word. She has written over 80 manuscripts - all historical and centering on couples finding love and a happy ever after together.

http://www.authorsusanpayne.com

Email: authorspayne@gmail.com